"I don't find
Jared."

"You used to."

"You're being ridiculous." Peyton sounded miffed.

He rolled on top of her and braced his arms on either side of her hips, trapping her. "Am I?" He made the mistake of looking at her mouth just as her tongue moistened her lips again. "Then why won't you give me a straight answer?"

"I'm not hiding from anything. The past couple of days have been miserable and I'm exhausted. Would you please leave?"

Jared wasn't buying it. He leaned forward and cupped her cheek in his palm, smoothing his thumb along the satiny softness. Her breath caught.

"Don't do this, Jared." Her whispered words were more invitation than rejection.

"Why? What are you afraid of?" He nibbled her earlobe and she trembled. With agonizing slowness, he tasted his way down her throat. He stopped just below her lips. "Just that you won't stop me if I do this?"

Peyton's soft moan of pleasure when his mouth caught hers in a hot openmouthed kiss was all the answer he needed.

Dear Reader,

I'd like to thank everyone who took the time out of their busy schedules to write me about my October 2001 Harlequin Blaze novel, *Sleeping with the Enemy* (#10). Chase and Dee's romance is a book that will always be special to me, and to hear from you that you also enjoyed their story has been one of the many highlights of my career.

As promised, I now offer you Jared and Peyton's rocky road to romance, in *Seduced by the Enemy*. It is my hope that you will enjoy their story, and find that I kept my promise by bringing you a sexy, suspenseful tale of romance and intrigue.

I so enjoy hearing from readers. Feel free to drop me a line anytime at P.O. Box 224, Mohall, ND 58761 or by visiting my Web site at www.jamiedenton.net.

Until next time,

Jamie Denton

P.S. Don't forget to check out tryblaze.com!

Books by Jamie Denton

SEDUCED BY THE ENEMY

Jamie Denton

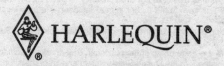

HARLEQUIN®

TORONTO • NEW YORK • LONDON
AMSTERDAM • PARIS • SYDNEY • HAMBURG
STOCKHOLM • ATHENS • TOKYO • MILAN • MADRID
PRAGUE • WARSAW • BUDAPEST • AUCKLAND

For Leena.
Fate brought us together,
Friendship keeps us that way.
Always,
Jamie

ISBN 0-373-79045-7

SEDUCED BY THE ENEMY

This edition published by arrangement with Harlequin Books S.A.

® and TM are trademarks of the publisher. Trademarks indicated with ® are registered in the United States Patent and Trademark Office, the Canadian Trade Marks Office and in other countries.

Visit us at www.eHarlequin.com

Printed in U.S.A.

1

TIME WAS RUNNING OUT.

He'd have to make his move soon before *they* figured out he'd been hiding right under their noses for the past week. He kept his movements to the darkness of night, primarily because doing so had become so familiar. In fact, the night had been his constant companion for far too long, but it kept him cloaked in the fantasy of security. A false sense of security, true, but one he understood and respected. His survival instincts, which had failed him only once in the three years he'd been on the run, were once again at a peak. Instincts made even sharper now as he stood in the shadows outside *her* home. The home of the woman who had handed him over to the bureau as if they'd never been in love. A woman he could no longer trust, but who would have to trust him if she wanted to stay alive.

Jared Romine blew out a stream of smoke from the cheap, generic cigarette, then tossed the butt into the gutter. He was alive, and that had to count for something. At least lately it did.

He stuffed his hands into the pockets of the well-worn, leather bomber jacket, his fingers finding the key to the low-rent motel room he'd checked into for the week. Thanks to fellow agent Chase Bracken, and the manila envelope tucked between the mattress and the box springs back at the room, he was that much closer to the truth that would finally free him, that would finally allow him to reclaim his life. He'd once foolishly believed he could have the semblance of a normal life, but the cost of that error in judgment had been astronomical. It was a lesson he'd not soon forget.

He leaned against the gnarled trunk of the leafy tree outside her home, while his instincts shouted at him that the perfect opportunity would soon be at hand. Timing would be everything, but he wouldn't, *couldn't,* make a move until the optimum moment.

In the meantime, patience was key. Something he'd had plenty of experience with, a desire to stay alive. Both had kept him one step ahead of a series of federal agents on his trail. He might not be on the Federal Bureau of Investigation's most-wanted list, but he was definitely their biggest embarrassment, and that was as good as having a price on his head, with a big red Dead Or Alive stamped across a wanted poster.

He'd defied them by staying ahead of the supposed good guys. By drifting from one small town to another, losing himself in large cities. And until his one fatal mistake, he'd never stayed in one place for too long. Careful never to draw too much attention to himself, he worked whatever jobs he could find to provide himself with basic sustenance and the bare minimum in creature comforts. Creating a new identity each time he moved, he searched relentlessly for the truth— and continued to slam up against one brick wall after another.

Thanks to Chase Bracken, the undercover agent

who'd fallen in love with his younger sister, Dee, Jared finally had been handed the truth. At least a part of it. He prayed it was enough.

Time was running out.

Once the wheels that were set into motion started to grind, it would be too late. For him. And for *her*.

At one time he'd been a highly trained deep-cover agent for the FBI. They'd trained him how to hide. As a former Naval Intelligence officer, reinventing himself and creating opportunity where none existed was second nature; they were skills that had served him as well as they'd hampered him since he'd gone underground. Thank God it was all going to end soon.

To anyone who might happen to gaze out their pretty curtained window on this sultry Indian summer night, he was nothing but a neighbor who'd stepped outside for a smoke. Nothing unusual. Nothing to draw too much attention to himself in the modest Arlington, Virginia, residential district where the neighbors kept to themselves.

He waited and watched.

His time was nearly up.

He'd been standing in the shadow of the tree for almost thirty minutes, and it was now close to midnight. Any longer and his presence might raise suspicion. He knew where she lived. He could come back again if it became necessary. Still he waited outside her house, shifting his gaze from the surrounding area to her bedroom window and the moderately priced sedan parked in the drive of her moderately priced home. The perfect life she'd always wanted for herself.

Once upon a time, it would have been *their* perfect life.

No lights shone through the windows of her perfect little house in the suburbs. Was she sleeping, or sitting in bed reading some brief she'd brought home from the office? He envisioned her curled beneath the sheets of the bed they'd once shared, with one hand tucked beneath her chin and the other hidden beneath the mound of pillows she insisted on having, but rarely used. Did she still sleep in worn flannel pajama bottoms and a skimpy tank top that barely reached her navel? Had she stopped reaching out for him in the middle of the night when she'd had a bad dream? After all the time that had passed, undoubtedly.

He heard the slamming of a screen door and stepped deeper into the shadows. Peering cautiously around the tree trunk, he watched as a portly, middle-aged man in a bathrobe and slippers stepped off the porch of the house directly across the street. Seconds later a light flared, followed by the steady red glow from a cigarette.

"Hurry it up, Henley," the guy said to the small, scruffy white dog who'd accompanied his owner out into the warm, sultry night.

Henley darted off to a neighbor's yard to leave his calling card. The dog took a dump and the heavyset guy chuckled. "Good work, boy. That'll teach that old bat to let her cat dig in the missus's flower beds."

Henley finished his business, then pricked his ears forward. The dog's attention zeroed in on the tree Jared hid behind.

Damn.

He couldn't make his move now. He'd have to wait

until there was little or no chance of him being spotted entering her home. He'd have to remain patient for just a little while longer. Except he didn't have a lot of time left. If his instincts and Chase were right, the whole mess was close to blowing up and taking with it another person he'd once cared for deeply. The woman who'd betrayed him.

When he'd met with Chase and Dee four weeks ago, he'd realized they were unaware of the fact that *she'd* turned him over to the feds. After reading the information he'd found in the case file, Chase had suspected a no follow-up order had been issued. Which confirmed Jared's own suspicions that whoever was involved in framing him was pretty high up the ladder in the bureau, based on the lack of information regarding *her* involvement in their failed attempt to arrest him.

Henley must've decided there was no threat. The dog ran back to his owner and together they entered the house.

Jared turned and headed down the quiet side street. He'd been coming here for a week, watching and waiting. Other than himself, no one else was conducting surveillance on her, of that much he was certain.

Now he knew what he had to do. She was predictable, except for tonight, when she'd arrived home after eleven. Usually she left her office no later than seven-thirty and was home by half past eight, nine at the absolute latest.

Tomorrow he'd make his move, because time was running out.

PEYTON DOUGLAS SNAPPED the heavy volume of federal codes and procedures closed with a disgruntled sigh. The thick lexicon hadn't contained the information she'd been hoping to find, but the Justice Department had an extensive law library at their counsels' disposal, where she hoped she'd find the answers...eventually.

U.S. v. Howell wasn't supposed to be a difficult case. It should have been a slam dunk for the Justice Department, except for that nasty business about a Fourth Amendment violation by the Drug Enforcement Agency credited with busting Howell. A rookie mistake by a seasoned agent that frustrated her, because the agent in question knew better. If she couldn't turn this case around by winning her argument against defense counsel's motion to suppress evidence, Howell could very well walk right back to the street, where coordinating large scale heroine deals was his way of life, instead of doing ten to twenty in a federal prison as he deserved.

A quick glance at her thin, gold wristwatch told her it was time to go home. She never stayed in the office past seven-thirty if she could help it. Tonight, instead of shutting down her computer and doing just that, she slipped the defense motion from the file and started reading...again. She'd already put in a long week, spending more time in court than in the office, where she needed to prepare for the upcoming Howell motion. At least she had the weekend to continue her research. Maybe she should call it a night and come back early in the morning, she thought, then kept reading the defense motion.

The truth was she enjoyed her Saturday mornings

in the office, when the hallowed halls of the Justice Department were unusually silent. More often than not, she did some of her best work on those quiet mornings when the only sounds that could be heard were the occasional radio broadcast from the office of another junior attorney, or the gentle hum of her own computer. What she really enjoyed was being alone with all that history within the sacred halls of justice. One Saturday morning a few years ago she'd ventured into the old case files room and spent the entire morning and half the afternoon reading dusty old court transcripts and files involving some of the biggest mobsters from the thirties and forties. They were the stuff old gangster movies were made of, but a thousand times more colorful and twice as deadly as their Hollywood depictions. What she wouldn't have given to be around back then, to be the lawyer who finally brought the big guys like Al Capone and his equally evil counterparts to justice.

"I'm calling it a night just as soon as I finish up your research notes for the Points and Authorities," her secretary, Kellie Nicols, said from the doorway, interrupting Peyton's delusions of grandeur. "Do you need me to come in tomorrow to work on the reply to the Howell motion?"

Peyton glanced up at her secretary. She'd worked with Kellie since her first day in the Justice Department four years ago. The two women had hit it off right away and were more friends than boss and employee. In fact, there was only one other person who knew her as well as Kellie, and as much as Peyton swore she wouldn't think about him, he'd steal into her mind at the oddest times, leaving her with a deep sense of melancholy and regret.

"No," she answered with a shake of her head, hoping to dislodge thoughts of Jared Romine just as easily. "You have a life. Go live it."

Kellie grinned, her brilliant green eyes sparkling with laughter as she crossed the room. She smoothed her short black skirt before she sat in one of the chairs in front of Peyton's desk. "Who told you that line of garbage? I'm single, I live alone with two cats and have no potential prospects on the horizon. How pathetic is that?"

Peyton leaned back in the warm leather executive chair and slipped off her reading glasses. "You're twenty-eight years old, Kel, not eighty-eight. I wouldn't exactly call you a spinster."

Kellie laughed while she pulled the pins from her hair, letting the auburn waves fall around her shoulders. "My downstairs neighbor, Mrs. Markum, is sixty-seven years old. She has more dates than I do. And she doesn't own any cats, either. It's Friday night and where am I? Typing up research notes for Points and Authorities on a case we're probably going to lose. Pathetic, I tell you. Just pathetic."

"I didn't ask you to stay," Peyton retorted with a grin. "And what makes you think we're going to lose Howell?"

Kellie shrugged. "Gut instinct. The Fourth Amendment's a hard one to get around, and that agent definitely blew it big time. Sorry, Counselor. There's just no way around something like this. And from the notes I've already typed, you agree with me."

"Don't I usually." Peyton really couldn't argue.

She'd been feeling the same way since her direct supervisor, Bradley Jacobs, had handed her the case last week. "I hate to let Howell walk, though. He's one of the bad guys that really deserves to be behind bars."

Kellie shrugged her slender shoulders again. "Win some, lose some. Now, let me see that rock again."

A slow grin touched Peyton's mouth. "You've seen it a dozen times today already."

"So, what's one more? It's gorgeous, Peyton," Kellie said, standing. "If someone like Leland Atwood had just given me a two-carat-diamond engagement ring, you can bet I'd be shoving that puppy under everyone's nose for them to admire."

Peyton laughed and allowed Kellie to lift her hand so she could get a closer look at the emerald-cut diamond solitaire Leland had given her last night, when she'd finally accepted his proposal of marriage. Now that she'd said yes, she still couldn't explain why she'd waited. It wasn't that she didn't love Leland. She admired him and respected him, two elements she knew would make their marriage a comfortable one. Leland wasn't the type to run at the first sign of trouble, either. He was the kind of man who was committed to anything he chose to accomplish.

A former Justice Department attorney himself, he'd left the DOJ to accept an appointment as a federal court judge shortly after Peyton joined the department. Leland's career was definitely on the fast tract, as evidenced three years later with an appointment to the federal appellate court as a circuit court justice. His goal was to one day make it to the Federal Supreme

Court. Peyton had little doubt Leland would one day realize his dream.

With all his potential, she should have found the decision to marry him an easier one to make. He had a bright future ahead of him as a relatively new appointee to the appellate court, and at thirty-nine he kept in shape by playing racquetball twice a week and jogging five miles daily regardless of the weather. But for reasons Peyton couldn't pinpoint, every time he'd asked her to marry him during the last two months, she'd hesitated, claiming she wasn't sure if she was ready to settle down.

Settle down? she silently scoffed. Her work was her life. What was there to settle down? She didn't own a cat, or even so much as a goldfish. About the only wild oats she'd ever sown were the ones she sprinkled with salt and a little butter in her cereal bowl each morning.

It hadn't always been that way, she mused. Once upon a time, she had had a great love affair. One man had stolen into her heart, into her soul, but it had ended badly, as great affairs often do. Except most didn't end with one of them turning the other over to law enforcement.

"You're lucky, Peyton. Most people find a great love only once," Kellie said, as if reading her mind. "You've had it twice."

Peyton pulled her hand free, feeling suddenly uncomfortable. "Jared was a mistake. Leland and I are much more suited to each other."

Kellie frowned down at her. "But you're in love with him, right? I mean, he's obviously in love with you. Two carats' worth."

"I love Leland, yes. He's gentle and kind, and he appreciates me the way I am. He isn't always trying to change me, to get me to loosen up and live life on the edge. Leland is…comfortable, and that's something I need in my life."

"Comfortable, or safe?" Kellie challenged.

"Is there a difference?"

Kellie walked to the window overlooking the busy street ten floors below, and stared out into the darkness for a moment. "Do you want to know what I think?" she asked, keeping her back to Peyton.

"Not really, but I have a feeling you're going to tell me, anyway."

Kellie turned to face her, a frown marring her delicate, petite features. "Leland's safe, Peyton. He doesn't make you feel too much. Not like…well, not like Jared."

Peyton let out a slow breath. She'd been thinking about Jared, and now Kellie was reminding her of what she'd tried for three long years to forget but could never quite completely manage to do.

Her friend knew how difficult it had been for her when she'd made the phone call to turn Jared over to the bureau. But he'd gotten away, knowing she was the one to betray him. She hadn't wanted to believe him capable of a brutal double murder or of stealing two million dollars, but the agents who'd come to see her had shown her the evidence against him. As an attorney for the United States, reviewing evidence and building a case out of that evidence was her job—a job she did damn well, if her recent promotion was any indication. And she'd seen more than enough to know there was little remaining doubt of Jared's guilt.

He'd claimed he'd been framed, but what she'd seen with her own eyes told another story. The story of Special Agent Jared Romine, one of the Federal Bureau of Investigation's best turned bad.

The truth was indeed damning. Jared's fingerprints had been all over the crime scene. From everything she'd been shown, the evidence not only pointed solely at Jared as the shooter, but as the one who'd taken the two million in cash from Senator Martin Phipps's office, as well. She still hadn't understood why the senator had had that kind of money lying around, and she probably never would know. Still, while her mind understood that everything pointed to Jared as the guilty party, her heart had taken a whole lot longer wrapping itself around the fact that he'd actually killed his partner, Jack Dysert, and the senator's top aide, Roland Santiago. Two million bucks was a hell of a motivator, so maybe she had her answer, after all.

She looked at the solemn expression on Kellie's face, at the compassion and understanding shining in her eyes. Kellie never judged. She only offered support and comfort. As far as friends went, she was easily Peyton's closest and dearest.

Peyton stood. "I won't deny it. On a certain level, yes, Leland does make me feel safe." She stuffed the Howell motion back into the file before turning off her laptop, wishing she could shut down thoughts of Jared just as easily. "And yeah, I guess you could say *he* is safe, too. He's got a solid career ahead of him. We have the same goals. We're well suited. There's nothing wrong with that, Kel. Not if it's what I want."

Kellie let out a long breath, her gaze filling with

frustration. "What about passion? I mean, okay, I like Leland. He's a nice enough guy and he obviously adores you, but come on, Peyton. The guy just screams beige."

Peyton frowned. "Beige?"

"Yeah. Beige. You know, you're making love with the guy and he's feeling a little adventurous so he lets you be on top. But he's not looking at you, he's staring at the ceiling, and instead of saying something wicked and naughty that'll excite you more, he says, 'I think we should paint the ceiling beige.'"

Peyton couldn't help herself; she laughed. "Okay, so Leland is a little conservative. But for the record, Ms. Nicols, there's nothing wrong with beige. Beige is a nice, neutral color. It goes with just about everything."

"Beige is *boring*," Kellie countered. "I just don't want you to settle for beige and then find out later you really wanted shocking blue or hot and sexy red."

Her days of hot and sexy red were over. Peyton knew that, and embraced the staid, stable life she'd created for herself. She'd betrayed hot and sexy red and had made up her mind to opt for safe, secure and settled. The betrayal held a wealth of regret, but she'd had no other choice. If she thought about it, she was glad she'd finally made the decision to marry Leland, even if it had taken her two months to accept his proposal. She'd made the right choice. Wasn't that what mattered in the long run? That'd she'd made the choice that was right for her?

Peyton slid her laptop into her briefcase, then considered adding the Howell file. Leland was away for the weekend at a judges conference, and chances were all she'd do tonight was more research, anyway, so she moved the file to the side of her desk. Since she'd be in the office tomorrow morning, there was no sense dragging it home with her.

She snapped her briefcase closed. "Hot and sexy red is you, Kel. Not me."

Kellie planted her hands on her slender hips. "When I first met you, you could be classified as hot and sexy red." She held up her hand to stop the argument hovering on Peyton's lips. "I know, I know. That's the past. Beige is safe. Boring, but safe. Just make sure Leland is what you really want, okay?"

Peyton set the briefcase on her chair to shrug into her navy blazer. "It is," she said, adjusting the collar. "*He* is, okay?"

Kellie let out a long-suffering sigh. "Okay," she said, but her eyes told another story, and Peyton didn't want to look close enough to read the words. She didn't need to. She had them memorized, and knew the story hadn't equaled the stuff fairy tales were made of, but a cold, hard reality with a different ending, one filled with betrayal and heartache. A tale that told the story of a man and a woman who'd been made for each other, until one of them had taken a path the other could never follow.

"Come on," Peyton said, leading the way out of her office. "I'll walk you out."

Kellie sat down at her desk just outside Peyton's office and pulled the research notes she'd typed from the printer. "You go on ahead. I'm staying in the city this weekend, so I'm going to finish these Points and Authorities before I leave. I get to meet dear old mom for a late dinner, and then it's back to her place for a girls' weekend," she said, then shuddered dramatically. "I told you my life was pathetic."

"At least you have a family who cares about you," Peyton said, shifting her briefcase to her other hand.

"Yeah, too much. My weekend will consist of hearing ad nauseam what a perfect life my older sister, Monica, has with her perfect husband, perfect children and perfect house. Even her precision trained German shepherd is perfect. Oh yeah, and when am I going to find the perfect man, yada, yada, yada. Still sound like loads of fun?"

Peyton laughed and pulled her keys from her purse. "You know you love it. Have fun," she said, then started toward the exit. "I'll see you Monday after the Howell hearing."

Since there were few people left in the building so late on a Friday night, it was no wonder the parking garage was practically deserted when she stepped off the elevator. Gripping her briefcase in her left hand, she positioned her keys in her right as a paltry weapon against any would-be mugger. She crossed the parking garage, listening for sounds other than the click of her own sensible navy pumps against the concrete.

The light nearest her car was still burned out, deepening the shadows as she approached her Ford Taurus. The light had been out since Monday. She made a mental note to have Kellie advise the building superintendent of the problem again. It really wasn't safe to be waltzing through the parking garage at night, but doing so without adequate lighting was just plain stupid.

Having no other choice, she approached her car using a great deal of caution. She opened the trunk and placed her briefcase inside, then, after a cursory glance around the area, slammed the trunk closed and pressed the button on her remote to unlock the door. Out of habit, she looked through the rear driver's side window, but it was an exercise in futility, since the interior lamp in the car had obviously chosen to burn out, as well. What was it with her and lightbulbs lately?

She slipped into the car, slid the key into the ignition and turned it over before reaching up to pull the seat belt in place. Her hand stilled in midair and a scream lodged in her throat when a large, callused hand covered her mouth. Then something hard and round was pressed against the base of her skull.

2

"HELLO, PEYTON."

She'd recognize that voice anywhere. Deep, and as smooth as the highest quality brandy. Even though she detected a hardness in his tone she didn't remember, there was no mistaking it was him.

Jared.

He'd come back. For her? For revenge? Considering she'd turned him in once, coupled with the fact that he was holding a gun to the back of her head, she wasn't about to make any snap decisions about his motivation for returning.

She inhaled slowly and fought to exhale evenly in an effort to still the rapid cadence of her heart. Fear-induced panic would do her no good and would have her thoughts scattering like autumn leaves dancing in a wind storm. Focus and concentration had to be her sole objectives if she had any hope of escaping him, and maybe even learning what he wanted from her and why he'd come back.

"Let's just take things slow and easy," he said, his voice low, as if he was talking to her over a candle-light dinner and not holding her hostage in her own car. "No one needs to get hurt."

Not getting hurt was just fine by her. Slow and easy would give her time to think, to take advantage of the first opportunity to escape and call the authorities. He wasn't the same man she'd once loved, and she desperately needed to remember that, instead of exhuming memories better left buried. The man holding her captive was the enemy, and dangerous. A fugitive who'd murdered his partner and the top aide to a prominent United States senator, and made off with two million dollars like it was some grand prize for his horrendous crime. Since she was the one who'd attempted to hand him over to the feds on a silver platter, she had a right to be fearful and cautious.

She remained perfectly still, concentrated on breathing evenly, and slowly opened her eyes, only to peer into the shadowed darkness of the deserted parking garage.

"Listen carefully, Peyton." He reminded her exactly who was in charge by adding the slightest amount of pressure with the weapon he held on her.

As if she needed reminding.

"Put your hands on the steering wheel."

In the rearview mirror, she sought him out, but the darkness inside the vehicle prevented her from discerning anything more than the reflection of his silhouette. She wanted, *needed* to see his eyes. For as long as they'd been together, she'd always been able to read him by the look in his eyes. It'd been the only way she'd known when he was upset, frustrated, even angry. She'd also known the love he'd once felt for her was as real as it got.

And when she'd betrayed him, she'd known how deeply she'd hurt him.

Those days were long gone. But that knowledge didn't stop her need to look into his dark emerald eyes now when it was most important, when one glance would tell her whether or not she was in real danger. The blasted darkness prevented her from searching for the truth.

He kept his hand over her mouth so she couldn't scream bloody murder. Not that anyone would hear her this time of night in the deserted parking garage, but just the same, he obviously wasn't about to take any chances.

Her eyes darted to the steering wheel, then back to the rearview mirror. "Forget it, Peyton." The silky tone of his voice stirred memories she couldn't afford to think about now.

How he could see so clearly when she could barely make out the shape of his head was beyond her.

"I disconnected the horn." He added a little more pressure with the weapon. "Hands, sweetheart. Steering wheel." He nudged again. "Now."

Sudden anger reared up inside her, white-hot and fiery, shoving aside her earlier fear and uncertainty. She did as he ordered, then tried to twist her head free of his grasp. A useless endeavor. He held her head firmly against the headrest and what she was certain was the nose of a pistol. Frustration nipped at her when she couldn't even open her mouth to bite his hand.

"Take it easy, sweetheart. I'm not here to hurt you, but to save you."

Save me? From whom? she wanted to rail at him. *Or what?*

"This car has automatic locks, right?" he asked her, instead of answering the question she couldn't voice.

She nodded her head as much as his tight hold would allow.

"We're gonna do this slow and easy," he repeated. "I don't want to hurt you, but I will if I have to, if it'll keep you safe. Do you understand that, Peyton?"

He waited, so she nodded again.

"Good. I'll explain everything later, but right now, I want you to reach over and engage the locks."

None of what he was telling her made sense. Keep her safe? As far as she could tell, he posed the only danger. Didn't he realize that after what he'd done, he could end up being shot on sight? He was a wanted man, for crying out loud.

Once she hit the button and the locks clicked, he finally removed the pressure from the weapon he held on her. She heard the rustle of fabric and assumed he'd stuffed the gun into his pocket.

Breathing suddenly became a whole lot easier.

"I'm going to remove my hand. Are you going to scream?"

She shook her head. No one would hear her, anyway. She seriously doubted the aging guard could hear her if he was standing directly in front of her. Still, she had to do something. Was she really supposed to believe she was the one in danger, when it was his face on a wanted poster?

With his hand still clamped over her mouth, he reached over and snagged her purse off the seat, dropping it on the floorboard beside him.

"I'm going to remove my hand. Scream, and who knows what might happen. I'm feeling a little edgy right now, so I wouldn't make any fast moves if I were you. You understand me, sweetheart?"

At her nod, he added, "Okay. Ease over to the passenger seat."

As slowly as he'd ordered her to follow his instructions, he removed his hand. She sucked a large gulp of air into her lungs. "What do you think you're doing?" she snapped at him, ignoring his demands. "Why are you here?"

"Now that's a hell of a greeting for someone you haven't seen in three years," he said, his voice dripping with sarcasm. "Move over."

Remaining behind the wheel, she shifted in the seat so she could get a good look at him. Shock coursed through her at the sight. Although vibrantly alive, and way too virile for her not to notice, he'd aged. A lot more than three years would warrant if he hadn't been hiding from the authorities, and doing only God knew what to stay alive and hidden. Thanks to the lights on the dash, she could just make out haggard lines of fatigue bracketing his eyes and the slight gray sprinkled along his temples. He was only two years older than her thirty-one years, but he looked so much older, and tired, as if he hadn't had a good night's rest in weeks, maybe even months.

Three years, her conscience reminded her. *Three long, no doubt hellish, years.*

Against her better judgment, compassion nipped at her. She desperately wanted to feel nothing toward him, but deep down she knew she'd have an easier time asking for the moon to be personally delivered to her doorstep with a pretty pink ribbon wrapped around it. Jared had been such an important part of her life. He'd *been* her life, or so she'd thought once upon a time. Despite her need to remain detached, the trace of fear she detected in his gaze gave her heart a sharp tug. The Jared she'd known, the Jared she'd once loved with all her heart, had never been afraid of anything. That his eyes held even a hint of that emotion now worried her, even more so than the determination she sensed there, as well.

"You're a fugitive, Jared," she said, lowering her voice. "As an officer of the court, it's my duty to—"

"Save me your legal duty bullshit, Peyton," he said with an unmistakable hardness in his tone. "I've heard it before. Remember? Now move it over like I told you to, real slow."

She had to find a way to get through to him. Certainly he realized the danger of even being in the D.C. area. If he was found, they'd kill him. She knew that. She'd been involved with Jared long enough to know feds didn't take too kindly to their own going south, much less killing a fellow agent in the line of duty.

"They're looking for you, Jared. They're *always* looking for you."

"Tell me something new," he said impatiently. "Now move it."

She twisted around and acted before she could think about the possible consequences. She slammed the car into reverse and stepped hard on the gas. The car shot backward, tires squealing on the smooth concrete. Jared swore vividly and scrambled to keep upright. She jerked the car to a hard stop, but before she could shift into Drive, he reached over the seat and killed the engine. As he tried to remove the keys, she fought him, tugging unsuccessfully on his hands, pulling on the sleeve of his lightweight jacket. He yanked the keys from the ignition and tossed them on the floor at her feet. She knew then the battle was lost.

Not ready to give up the fight completely, she made one last-ditch effort and reached for the door, opened it, but he swore again and grabbed a handful of her hair. The butterfly clip holding it in place flew to God knew where an instant before her feet hit the pavement. *Dammit!*

For a few moments, the only sound inside the car was their ragged breathing. In the distance, she could hear the sounds of the D.C. traffic. "That's the wrong way, sweetheart," he said, his mouth dangerously close to her ear. His warm breath fanned her flushed skin and sent a shiver traveling down her spine. "Close the door, Peyton."

Temporarily out of viable escape options, she reluctantly did as he ordered. She tried to pull away from him, away from that mouth close enough to brush against her skin, but he held on tight.

"Look, if it's the car you want," she said, struggling to calm herself, "just let me get my briefcase and you can have it."

"So you can run to the nearest phone and report it stolen? Not a chance, sweetheart."

"Stop calling me that," she told him. She was no longer his sweetheart, babe or any of the other silly endearments he'd used during their affair. "What do you want?"

"Dammit, I'm trying to protect you, Peyton."

"Then you should have stayed away."

"I couldn't. This is what they wanted."

"What who wanted? You're talking in circles."

"Look, I'll explain later. Right now we need to get out of here. They could be watching us even now."

"Who, Jared?" She wanted to understand, but without an explanation, she was reduced to guessing games. "Who could be watching? The bureau? They wouldn't be watching, they'd be surrounding the car with guns drawn like a bunch of liquored-up farmers on a turkey shoot. And guess who the turkey is?"

He let out a frustrated breath. "Let's take this back to the beginning, okay? Move over to the passenger seat."

"I'm not moving anywhere until you explain what's going on."

"I told you—I'll explain later." The words were sharp and clipped. "Move it, Peyton. Now!"

With nothing left to do but follow his orders, she eased over to the passenger seat. He kept her hair wrapped around his hand until he moved first one, then the other leg over the seat and slid behind the wheel. He adjusted the seat to fit his long, powerful legs, then adjusted the mirror and double-checked the locks. He even made sure the window lock was engaged before he scooped up the keys and started the car. With his foot on the brake and his hand on the gearshift, he turned to look at her. "I'm not going to hurt you."

"Oh, really?" Although his gaze held sincerity, she still balked. She was effectively his captive. He was the one in control, the one calling the shots, and she hated it almost as much as she hated the changes in him. "Then what do you call that gun you held to my head? A greeting card?"

He had the audacity to offer her a sheepish grin as

he reached into his pocket. When he opened his hand, she stared in disbelief at the round, black plastic object lying across his calloused palm. "A lighter? You mean to tell me you scared me half to death with a disposable lighter?"

He slipped the car into Drive and headed toward the exit. "It worked, didn't it?" He stuffed the lighter back into his pocket and pulled out something else.

She looked down at his hand. "I suppose you're going to tell me you're responsible for the light being out in the parking garage, too," she said, taking the small lightbulb from his palm to return it to the over-head lamp in the car.

When he just grinned at her again, she let out a disgusted sigh, then reached behind her to pull the seat belt into place. Being kidnapped was one thing, but that didn't mean she had to compound stupidity by riding around unprotected. "Will you at least tell me where we're going?"

"Somewhere that's safe." He glanced quickly in her direction. "At least for now."

"And then you'll let me know what this is all about?"

"Yeah, Peyton. I'll tell you. But I guarantee you're not going to like it."

HE LOVED HIS JOB. He was powerful, connected and damn good at what he did. Invitations to dinner parties in the homes of Washington's movers and shakers always came to him. The other senatorial aides on the hill called on him for advice and counsel. Lobbyists vied for his attention and were grateful when he gave it to them. Visits to the White House were a common part of his job, and the rush of adrenaline he felt stepping into the hallowed halls of the West Wing, of having the ear of those closest to the president, never failed to lift him a little higher in his own self-esteem. He wasn't feared, but he was deeply respected, and respect meant everything to a man who'd crawled out of a dirt-poor childhood, one small step ahead of being trailer trash.

His father had been a drunk who'd died instantly behind the wheel of a battered pickup held together by lube oil, dust and a prayer, when it kissed the trunk of a tree at 60 mph. For reasons he failed to comprehend, his mother had mourned the death of her mean bastard of a husband and committed suicide three months later. Only thirteen at the time, thin, pale and oddly quiet, Stevie Radgetz had been the one to find his mother, along with an empty bottle of tequila and prescription sleeping pills as her companions in bed.

He'd gone to live with his father's brother, William Radgetz, following his mother's funeral. His drunken father and suicidal mother had been a picnic compared to dear old Uncle Willie. At least Stevie had known his parents had loved him in their own misguided way, even if it hadn't been enough for them to stick around. Willie didn't give a shit about him and didn't care who knew it, even thin, pale, dirty little Stevie. It was no secret the only reason Willie kept him around was for the government check that arrived each month, a check Stevie never saw so much as a penny of in the five years he lived in his uncle's ramshackle house on the edge of town. The only thing he'd ever seen from his uncle had been his fists when he'd had too much to drink, which was often.

A week after his eighteenth birthday, Stevie legally changed his last name to Radcliffe and left the Kentucky backwater town, never looking back. With the stash of money he'd earned from the few folks around town who would even hire a Radgetz to do their odd jobs, Steven Radcliffe made his way to California. A high-priced set of forged high-school transcripts and an honest college entrance exam score had enabled him to enroll at the University of California at Berkeley. Part-time jobs, a few of them unsavory, supported him in the lifestyle he'd dreamed of having. While the federal government funded his education with loans and grants, the college housed him first in a dorm and then in a frat house. He'd despised most of his frat brothers, with their spoiled ways and overindulgent parents. He wasn't stupid, however, and kept his disdain to himself while making the necessary contacts he knew he'd one day need to get his foot in the door of the life he so desperately craved. A life filled with wealth, position, and above all, respect.

His plan had been so simple, and was executed with ease. Any and all traces of dirty little Stevie Radgetz no longer existed. He'd gotten his first step in politics thanks to the father of one of his frat brothers, who'd introduced him to an up-and-coming politician. Steve made a name for himself in the political arena, but he never did have the desire to run for office himself. He was better suited behind the scenes, where the dealmaking took place, where the real power lay. Which was why one of the most revered senators on the hill, Senator Martin Phipps, an arrogant, pompous bastard, came to him to replace his former aide, the late Roland

Santiago. And why Steve was immediately called upon to clean up a very ugly mess.

The senator would trample his own grandmother if it meant getting ahead, and that suited Steve just fine. Hell, he'd even provide the running shoes, for the simple fact that when Phipps rose in power, Steve's own power and value increased. He liked that. A lot.

Quietly closing the door to his elegantly appointed office, he headed down the silent corridor to Phipps's office. Steve had news to impart, but he'd wisely waited until the offices were deserted, lest anyone overhear what he had to say.

The door stood ajar. Steve knocked once, stepped inside without waiting for an invitation and closed the door behind him. Phipps unnecessarily waved him in, said goodbye to his current mistress and hung up the phone.

"Rumor has it the president is going to announce the first appointment Monday morning," Steve said without preamble. Phipps liked getting straight to the point, while Steve always preferred a subtle approach. Shifting gears was as easy as playing to the senator's arrogance. Steve excelled in both.

Phipps stood and crossed the lush, jewel-toned Oriental rug to the carved armoire on the opposite end of the office. Keeping his back to Steve, he poured himself a Scotch, neat. "How much truth do you believe is behind the rumor?"

Steve carefully sat in the leather wing chair. "My source in the White House is extremely reliable."

"Good," Phipps said with a nod. He turned and smoothed his salt-and-pepper hair with his free hand, then grinned like the Cheshire cat. "I've been invited to Justice Elliot's farewell dinner. Beautifully ironic, wouldn't you say?''

''Only if the president appoints Galloway *and* Boswell to the bench once Middleton steps down,'' Steve reminded him. He felt confident the president would appoint the two federal appellate court judges to the bench of the United States Supreme Court. He also knew Phipps believed he held in his hands the power that would enable him to convince his fellow senators on the judiciary committee to vote in favor of the appointments. The truth was much more complicated.

''He will,'' Phipps answered arrogantly. ''First Galloway, and then Boswell in a few months, once Middleton announces his retirement.''

''*If* Middleton announces his retirement before the end of the session,'' Steve corrected.

Phipps ignored that comment. He moved from the armoire and propped his hip on the corner of his large oak desk. At sixty-two, Phipps was still athletically built and kept his body in shape. He worked out daily and was still as fit as he'd been during his years as the star quarterback at Texas A&M, followed by a brief stint in the pros.

Phipps's vibrant blue eyes filled with confident arrogance. ''They not only share the same party affiliation, but they openly supported the president's platform during the last election. With everyone focusing on the abortion issue again, they're the perfect choice.''

''You're very certain of this.''

''I'd bet your career on it, Radcliffe.''

No doubt he would, Steve thought. Phipps never

had any trouble getting what he wanted. Steve saw to it.

Phipps took a drink of the Scotch, then asked, "What else is on your mind, Radcliffe?"

Steve leaned forward and braced his elbows on his knees. "We've had a breach," he said, watching Phipps's expression intently. Confidence fled from the older man's eyes, replaced by a flash of fear, followed by anger.

"When?" the senator demanded.

"About a month ago."

"A month?" he roared.

Steve nodded.

"And why am I only just hearing of it?" Phipps lowered his voice.

"I only learned of it myself. I had a dinner meeting tonight with—"

"I don't give a rat's ass who you broke bread with," Phipps snapped. "What went wrong that we weren't notified immediately?"

Steve straightened. He'd expected the senator to be angry, but the fear in his eyes had taken him off guard. But then, when someone was trying to upset the balance of the Supreme Court, he suspected a little fear should be involved. The senator had a lot to lose. So did Steve, which was why he'd make sure the truth would never be leaked.

"Whoever did it was good," he told the senator. "We think it was a professional. He knew where to look and how to cover his tracks."

Phipps rose and started to pace. "Do you think it was him?"

"It's entirely possible, but I have my doubts."

"Enlighten me."

"He would've made a move by now if it'd been him."

Phipps let out a sigh. "We need to move first, before he does. Bring him out in the open, Radcliffe. You know what you need to do. It's time."

"Yes, Senator. I'll handle it." Steve stood and immediately headed for the door. He didn't have time to waste. He had another life to destroy.

3

TAKING THE HARD VINYL chair Jared indicated, Peyton sat at the round table in the far corner of the motel room and quickly surveyed her surroundings, surreptitiously searching for a means of escape. Her only hope was the bathroom, but from the brief glimpse she'd had when Jared flipped on the lights, she couldn't be sure if it even had a window. There had to be, she thought. Considering Jared had to have made getting out of places in a hurry his number one priority, she couldn't imagine him holing up without an alternate means of escape.

At least the place was clean, if a strong disinfectant smell was any indication. Although dull from years of wear and tear, the multicolored shag carpet was well maintained. Thankfully, she hadn't noticed a single critter scurrying from the light, either. Not that she cared one way or another, because she had no intention of staying.

The fact that he'd kidnapped her by disposable lighter, rather than gunpoint, reassured her to some small degree that regardless of all the tough talk, he didn't plan to hurt her. Still, a part of her wasn't quite so confident. In the hard man currently holding her captive, she barely recognized the Jared she'd known. Gone was the smooth, polished federal agent with a promising career ahead of him. A fugitive she barely recognized remained, one accused of a brutal double murder.

Only memories existed now. Memories better left alone if she planned to maintain emotional distance.

She watched him as he secured the door, then peered through a crack in the draperies to the parking lot they'd left only moments ago.

"So what do you plan on doing with me now that you've got me here?" She touched the tabletop with the tips of her fingers. When they didn't stick to the surface, she crossed her arms and leaned against the imitation wood grain. "If it's ransom money you're looking for, forget it. I'm practically broke."

He made a noise that could have been a grunt of disagreement. As if the security bar and dead bolt weren't enough, he slid one of the vinyl chairs beneath the knob and wedged it against the door.

"Jared? Are you going to tell me what's going on? I'd like to be home before midnight, if you don't mind."

He turned to face her. In the soft buttery glow of the lamplight, she finally saw him clearly. Unable to help herself, she stared in utter fascination. His dark mink-colored hair, always kept short, now brushed his collar, the perfect accompaniment to the faded jeans and worn denim shirt that stretched across his broad shoulders. There was that slight graying at his temples that conflicted with the rebel look, adding a distinguished quality that most men wouldn't see until their mid-forties or later. He was about twenty pounds thinner than she remembered, but from the way the jeans and shirt clung to his body, she suspected he was no less muscular. Maybe even more so.

Much to her surprise, she realized she longed to see the hint of mischief that had once filled his green eyes, along with the lopsided grin she could never resist. If she could catch just a trace of the old Jared, then maybe the past three years would all seem like a bad dream.

She gave herself a hard mental shake. The past could not be changed. Hadn't she learned that lesson time and again throughout her life? Reality stood before her, changed and unfamiliar. She might not like what he'd become, but the hardness she sensed had always lurked beneath the surface was now more apparent than ever before. He'd been an FBI agent, one of the best. An agent didn't regularly handle Black Ops or deep-cover assignments by not residing at the top of the pyramid. So what if his eyes looked her up and down now with glacial hardness? It made no difference to her whatsoever, even if it did make him even more handsome than she remembered. They were no longer simpatico. The part of her that had clung to the dream of happily-ever-after had died the day he turned his back on everything good and right.

Too bad none of her arguments could change one little fact of life—Jared Romine would always be able to turn her head.

As if he hadn't heard her questions or demands, he left his post by the door and crossed the room toward her.

"Jared. I want to go home," she repeated when he pulled his wallet from his hip pocket and tossed it on the nightstand along with her keys.

He looked at her over his shoulder. "Sweetheart, you can't go home. It's too dangerous."

The expression in his gaze rattled her. "So you've already said." She struggled to come to terms with the fear banked within the depths of his eyes. Fear for her? Or for himself when they caught him?

She pulled in a shaky breath and let it out slowly. The sooner she found out what he wanted, the sooner she could return to her life. To her safe existence, where beige was an exciting color.

"What's going on, Jared? If it's help you want—"

"Help?" Hardness replaced the anxiety in his eyes and he gave an abrupt bark of humorless laughter. "Oh, you'd help me all right. Straight into the gas chamber."

She shook her head. "You're not being fair."

He planted his hands on his hips and glared down at her. "Fair? You want fair?" His angry voice dripped with sarcasm. "How fair were you when you turned me over without even waiting to hear my side of the story?"

No, the night he'd come to her, she hadn't given him a chance to explain. If she had, they would've used whatever he'd told her against him. Her arms slid from the table. She balled her hands into tight fists, then stood and returned his glare with one of her own.

"They didn't give me a choice." The bitter taste of betrayal hadn't waned one iota in three years. "What did you want me to do, Jared? Risk being disbarred? Lose everything? After what they put me through, I think I paid a high enough price."

He let out a rough sigh and reached for her. "Look, I'm sorry."

Whether he was apologizing for being a jerk or for what her involvement with him had nearly cost her, she didn't know, and quite frankly, she was too ticked off at being kidnapped to really give a damn. She sidestepped him and made it to the nightstand to snag her keys. "It doesn't matter. I'm leaving. Don't waste your breath trying to change my mind."

"It's too dangerous for you now."

She faced him, anger and frustration still brewing inside her. "The way I see it, the only danger I'm in at the moment is a result of having been kidnapped by a fugitive. It's safer for both of us if I leave and pretend tonight never happened."

He narrowed the space between them. "It's not going to be that easy this time, Peyton."

The unexpected and sudden gentleness of his tone stroked her like a physical caress. Sweet, caring and way out of line. Damn Jared, and damn the memories swamping her. "It wasn't the last time, either."

She spun to leave, but before she took a single step toward freedom, he had her by the arm and used care to turn her around to face him. He wrapped his arm around her waist and pulled her close.

The feel of the long length of his body pressed against her was instant electricity. The urge to wreathe her arms around his neck and pull him down for a long, hot kiss overwhelmed her.

Now who's out of line?

"Let me go, Jared." Her nipples beaded and rasped against the lace of her bra, making a mockery of her demand.

That lopsided grin made an appearance, taking the edge off the hard angles of his face. "I remember a time when you didn't mind so much.'' The sensual darkening of his gaze matched the low, husky timbre of his velvety-smooth voice.

The insides of her thighs tingled in response, along with the first sensual tug of need pulling in her belly. "That was a long time ago. A lifetime ago.'' Obviously not long enough for her body to forget that heaven could always be found with Jared.

Oh, this was bad. Real bad. She had to get away from him. The last thing she needed was to complicate this mess any further. Stirring up wicked fantasies was not an option. Or worse, caving in to the desire weaving through her body. She set her hands against his shoulders and pushed.

Instead of letting her go, he tightened his hold, urging her body even closer. The soft denim of his jeans brushed against her legs, turning the tingling between her thighs to a demanding throb. Feeling the hard ridge of his fully erect penis pressing against his fly was like laying a match to a fuse of dynamite.

"Then why does it feel like I held you this way only yesterday?''

Probably because it felt that way to her, too, but she kept the traitorous thought to herself. "Why did you bring me here?''

Why did you have to come back into my life, even for a few hours?

"Answer me, Peyton.''

She wasn't going near that one, even if her life was in danger, as he claimed. "No. You answer my questions. You said once we were somewhere safe you'd tell me everything.''

He lifted his hand and smoothed his thumb along

her lower lip. "Your mouth has haunted my dreams for far too long."

"Jared," she replied. Whether in protest or invitation, she couldn't be sure. She wanted it to be protest, she really did, but the way her body was humming with anticipation, invitation was closer to the truth.

She stared, mesmerized, as he slowly dipped his head. The keys slipped from her fingers and clattered to the floor. Oh, mercy, he was going to kiss her. She knew she should stop him, but somewhere deep inside, some part of her that still clung to traitorous old memories ignored the necessary protests and outrage that would quickly put an end to the resurrection of the past. Instead, the second his lips brushed hers, her eyes closed and she welcomed the pressure of his mouth on hers.

She'd expected gentle. Maybe even tentative. But what began as the tender brushing of lips quickly evolved into something deeper and hotter and wetter than she'd experienced in a very long time. The last thing she anticipated was for need and desire to tear through her, causing every possible point of pleasure to pulse and throb.

As if the last three hellish years had never existed, she clung to him and gave herself up to the insistent pounding of desire as she slid her hands over his torso, exploring familiar territory. As if undressing Jared was still second nature to her, she quickly undid his shirt and smoothed her hands along his bare skin. The enticing flex of muscle and sinew beneath her fingertips had her sighing into his mouth.

An invitation didn't come any more engraved.

He responded by moving her backward until her

bottom came in contact with the textured wall. His heat surrounded her, engulfed her, and burned slow and hot, catching her completely off guard with its intensity. As though they'd never been separated, her body responded to his with the building of pleasure so overwhelming she knew she never wanted it to end.

His tongue stroked hers in a hot, erotic dance of seduction, sending tiny little tremors of pleasure dancing beneath her skin, igniting a hot flame that seared her from the inside out. Somewhere in the back of her mind she knew allowing them to continue was wrong, yet even the knowledge that she was charging down a forbidden path did nothing to stem the insistent need where she craved his touch the most. As much as her conscience screamed at her to push him away and put an end to this erotic nonsense, her heart yearned for the single moment in time where she could forget the past three years of loneliness, of longing for what could never be, of steeling herself against the hurt she'd seen in his eyes the night she'd betrayed him.

The kiss ended all too soon and he backed away from her. He shoved a hand through his hair and stared at her as if he'd never seen her before. Or maybe he was remembering another time, a time when they'd been in love.

Cool air brushed her skin, sending a chill down her spine. The desire to slip back into his arms, to feel the heat of his body pressing against hers, to reassure herself she wasn't suffering from another dream where she'd wake up to nothing but darkness and a deep ache in her chest, stunned her. She didn't know whether to weep with frustration or shout for joy that he was standing in front of her, holding her, kissing her, making her forget the horrendous pain after he'd run from the feds, leaving her behind to cope with the emotional and physical aftershocks from events that had spun out of control.

"That shouldn't have happened," he said, turning his back to her while he buttoned his shirt. "I apologize."

She shouldn't have let it happen, for a whole series of reasons, but she hadn't let it stop her from enjoying every second she'd been in his arms. It was only the shock of seeing him again, of knowing he was alive. Yeah, that made sense. She'd plastered herself all over him and kissed him as if it was the most natural thing in the world, just to reassure herself he wasn't a ghost of her imagination this time.

Now there was an argument she could *never* hope to sell to a jury.

"But it did happen," she heard herself saying. "And dammit, Jared, it felt right."

Was she insane?

Obviously.

He spun around to face her and stared in disbelief. "Right?" he said, after a half-dozen heartbeats of dead silence. He took a step toward her and snagged her left hand, lifting it until the engagement ring Leland had given her was between them. "Take a good look at that and then tell me again how *right* it felt."

There wasn't a single thing she could say in her defense, so she kept her mouth firmly shut. The absolute truth of it was she hadn't given Leland a solitary thought when she'd been wrapped around Jared. Did that make her a bad person? Maybe. Probably. But would a jury convict her because she'd lost her

head for a moment in the arms of the man who
touched her soul?

Without a doubt, she thought. She'd slipped. Made
a mistake. Her emotions were running in high gear
and she'd been momentarily rendered conscienceless.
No matter how right her heart and body had felt being
in Jared's arms, she wouldn't let something like that
happen again.

She hoped.

He let go of her hand. "That's what I thought," he
said, and moved away from her as if he couldn't stand
to be near her. He dropped into one of the vinyl chairs
at the round table and leaned back, lacing his fingers
together over his stomach. "So who is he?" he asked,
his tone conversational, as if he was asking whether
rain was expected in the forecast.

She bent to pick up the keys and set them on the
nightstand before answering. "Leland Atwood."

She returned to the table and sat across from Jared.
To someone who didn't know him as well as she did,
his impassive expression just might have been believ-
able, but there was a hardness in his eyes that belied
the boredom he attempted.

"Atwood?" He laughed, but the sound held more
bitterness than humor. "The pompous ass with the
DOJ? He's a good ten, twelve years older than you."

She folded her arms over her chest and gave him a
level stare. "Leland is not pompous, just conservative.
He's a federal court judge now, with the D.C. Circuit
Court."

"I don't care if he replaced Scalia on the high court,
he's still not your type. What do you see in him?"

She really didn't care much for Jared's sarcasm, but

history, maybe it was to be expected. type. Leland is kind, he works hard romising career ahead of him.''

whard,'' Jared said with a caustic laugh. of himself he can hardly fit through the door.

''He is not.'' So what if she sounded like a petulant child? This was her fiancé they were discussing, even if the entire conversation bordered on ludicrous.

A cocky grin canted his mouth. ''You'll get tired of him within a year.''

She didn't appreciate his smirk in the least. ''That just goes to show how little you know me.''

''Oh, I know you, sweetheart.'' He leaned forward suddenly and reached across the space separating them to rest his hand on her knee. Her skin tingled.

''I know you like it on top,'' he said in that low, husky voice normally reserved for late nights in front of the fireplace. ''I know you like it hot and nasty.''

She shoved his hand away, not because she didn't like him touching her, but she wasn't exactly thrilled that her body responded to him when she was engaged to marry another man. ''*That* was a long time ago. Besides, there's more to a marriage than great sex.''

He rested his hands on his knees and gave her a smug, I-know-better look. ''I'll bet Atwood doesn't make love to you like you need to be made love to, either. All you'll get out of him will be a duty fuck because it's the expected method of reproduction, not because it drives him crazy to see you go wild with desire. And not because he knows how to make you cry out with pleasure.''

She shot out of the chair and circled the bed.

"You're out of line, Jared. Way out of line. You don't know me anymore."

He was the second person in one day to make the same basic assessment of her fiancé. First her secretary and now Jared. Leland was a good man. He had staying power, and a strong sense of right and wrong. They didn't come any straighter than Leland Atwood.

"Within a year he'll have you knocked up and then you'll be lucky to get laid until he's deemed it's time for the next kid. The picture of the perfect family to show off to the world while he waits for an appointment to the Supreme Court," he continued. "And you'll go along with it because of some misguided sense of what happiness is, but you know what? You'll be dying inside. Little by little, the woman you were will disappear. Because Atwood, for all his drive to succeed, doesn't know a thing about the woman you are, or have the first clue about what you need."

She turned and looked at him as if he'd lost his mind. "Oh, and you do?"

That cocky grin was back for the sole purpose of setting her teeth on edge. "I never heard you complaining."

"That's because you were never around long enough," she retorted.

His grin faded and she felt a small sense of satisfaction.

"What are you saying?" he asked.

"Even before you...disappeared, you weren't around much." Weeks, sometimes months would go by without a single word from him. While she was at work, occasionally her mind would wander and she'd always send up a little prayer that he was safe. But the nights? Oh, those were the longest, and the hardest. When she had nothing else to occupy her mind, alone in bed with nothing but the darkness surrounding her, she'd envisioned one horrific scene after another until he came home again. They lived together for nearly a year before he ran, but in that time, she could probably count the weeks they'd actually been together on two hands.

"It was my job, Peyton. You know that."

"A job you never talked about. I knew what you did was dangerous, but you never once told me what it was you were doing when you'd be gone for weeks at a time."

God, why were they even having this conversation? What did it matter to her what Jared did? He no longer had that kind of hold on her.

"You know I couldn't talk about my assignments."

"Something, Jared. Anything would have been preferable to the constant fear and worry that you were never coming home. When you did finally disappear, it was almost a relief because I knew then that you wouldn't be back."

He came out of the chair and walked toward her, his eyes as thunderous as his expression. "You sure as hell didn't do anything to stop it. You invited the bastards into my own home. *Our* home."

Once again, they'd come full circle and were back at square one. Anger nipped at her and she snapped, "I didn't have a choice!"

"So you keep saying."

She balled her hands into tight fists and kept them at her side as she stared him down. "If I'd let you explain, if you'd told me anything, *anything*, it would have been used against you. They were going to charge you with murder, Jared. The kind that would have had you strapped down to a table with a needle in your arm and a big burly guard pressing a large round green button. I'm sorry, but once the death penalty has been carried out, there's no way to reverse it. And you are a prime candidate for lethal injection, based on the evidence I've seen.

"If I didn't cooperate, they could have prosecuted me for harboring, or aiding and abetting. We weren't married, we were only living together. Only a wife has the privilege of not testifying against her husband, which means *you* weren't afforded that protection under the law."

"I didn't kill Dysert or Santiago," he roared.

"So *you* keep saying," she shouted back. "But where's the evidence to the contrary? I'm a lawyer, Jared. A prosecutor for the United States. I know solid evidence when I see it."

He let out a harsh breath. "You think I'm guilty." He didn't question, he stated.

She sighed and fought for a calm she was nowhere near feeling. After he'd disappeared, she'd striven for order so she could survive yet another nightmare in her life. In a matter of hours, his presence had shot all her efforts for the past three years straight to hell.

No surprises. What a joke.

Nothing too emotional. Calm and serene had become painful and chaotic all over again.

"I don't know what to think." She struggled for an even tone. "You haven't told me anything. Nor have you told me why you brought me here." She lifted her hand to stop him from interrupting. "You keep saying it's dangerous for me, but how do you know that? Why would they come after me? As far as anyone knows, we haven't seen each other since the night you took off without a trace.''

''They're going to use you to get to me.''

''If that's true, then what are you doing here?'' she asked. ''Anywhere near me should be the last place you'd want to be.''

''I know what they're capable of,'' he said. He sat on the edge of the bed and looked up at her. Pain flashed in his eyes and her heart twisted. ''I'm here because I don't want anything to happen to you.''

She sat beside him and reached for his hand. ''It's been three years, Jared. It doesn't make sense that they'd bother with me now. Besides, after the first few months, the FBI finally left me alone. You didn't fail me, Jared. You failed yourself, and the law.''

He laced his fingers with hers. ''Yeah, it does make sense. This is a game I've played before. I failed then, but I swear to you, Peyton, I won't fail this time.''

Something in his voice frightened her. Whether it was the cold determination or the hollow sense of dread, she couldn't decide, but figured they both deserved equal attention. ''I don't understand.''

He turned his head to look at her. ''No,'' he said. ''It's not you I failed.''

Caution and dread warred inside her. Whatever he was about to tell her was big, that much she knew for certain. ''Then who?''

''My wife.''

4

"YOUR WIFE?"

Jared let out a rough sigh and wished he'd kept that part of his life to himself. Whether the desire to keep silent stemmed from not wanting to hurt Peyton— which didn't make a bit of sense, since she was engaged to the legal-ladder-climbing Atwood—or to save his own sorry hide a revisit of the guilt of Beth's murder, he couldn't be sure. Of one thing he was certain: telling Peyton about the woman he'd married just might convince her he was telling the truth about the danger she now faced.

"You're married?"

He hated that her voice was laced with pain almost as much as he despised the fact that she was questioning him when she'd given up that right the day she'd turned him in to the bureau. Besides, it wasn't as if she'd spent the past three years pining for him, considering she'd agreed to marry another man. Just one more notch on her belt of betrayal? Or jealousy she had no right feeling?

"Not any longer," he told her.

She stood and crossed the room before turning back to look at him. Her arms wrapped around her middle as if holding herself together. Combined with the hurt in her periwinkle eyes, she had his heart twisting behind his ribs. Damn.

More guilt? A sure bet, since he was becoming such a pro at it.

"I can't believe I'm hearing this." She shook her head as if to clear it. "You married someone."

The accusation in her voice that he'd betrayed *her* ticked him off. "Don't be a hypocrite, Peyton. That rock on your finger says you didn't wait around for me, either."

She looked at him as if he'd lost his mind, or as if her current premarital status didn't even belong in the conversation. "When did you have time to find yourself a wife *and* get a divorce?" She took a step backward, resting her bottom against the cheap, laminated dresser. "Why didn't they find you when you filed for divorce?"

A coldness crept into his veins that he couldn't have kept out of his voice if he'd wanted to...which he didn't. "Generally when one's wife is murdered, divorce isn't exactly a necessity."

Peyton's hands fell to her sides as she stared at him for what seemed like an eternity. "By whom?" she finally asked.

The doubt filling her eyes pushed that damned hot button again. "Who the hell do you think?" he snapped, coming off the bed toward her. The fact that she still believed him capable of murder chafed not only his pride, but had his heart stinging, as well. Once upon a time they'd meant the world to each other. Now she circled him like a hand-shy puppy.

She held her ground, though—he gave her credit for that much, especially considering she'd made a habit out of taking the path of least resistance whenever her personal life was involved.

"I wish I knew."

"Dammit, Peyton. You just can't trust me, can you?"

"You haven't given me much reason to." She fired the accusation back at him. She stood toe-to-toe with him, and dammit if the flash of heat in her eyes didn't have his gut clenching with what he recognized as desire. Guilt continued to nudge him, but he side-stepped it and clung to the anger simmering below the surface instead. Anger was good. It not only let him know he was still alive, but it gave him something else to concentrate on other than the need he had no right to feel.

He reached for her and held her upper arms in a tight grip. "You're going to have to learn. *Your* life depends on it."

She struggled, but he refused to let her go. The soft floral scent of her perfume teased his senses, threatening to slam him back to a time when angry words between them were about as common as a blizzard in August.

"The evidence against you is staggering," she argued. "And you haven't told me a damned thing since you dragged me here. If you want me to trust you, then start talking, Jared. And you can start by telling me who killed your wife."

"The same people that are now after you are responsible for Beth's murder."

As if he'd slapped her, she flinched, and something in her eyes died. "Her name was Beth?" she asked, her voice suddenly quiet.

He let go of her and his hands fell to his sides. "Yeah," he said, "her name was Beth." Sweet, caring Beth. Sadness weighed him down. She hadn't deserved to die. He might not have been the one to pull the trigger, but he was to blame for her death. All because he'd gotten tired, and been arrogant enough to believe that maybe they'd finally given up trying to find him.

He'd underestimated them, a mistake he would never make again.

"Was she very young?" Peyton asked.

He knew where this was going—straight down a path where the tracks were still fresh. Ignoring her questions was a possibility, but he understood that if he'd been completely honest with Beth, she might be alive today. A wrong he could never right.

He nodded before moving to the edge of the bed to sit. "She was only twenty-six."

The next question was inevitable. He could see it in Peyton's face when he looked up at her. The one that would compound the guilt he already felt, the one that would hurt them both when she asked it.

"Were you in love with her?"

A direct shot, right to the heart of the matter. No wonder she made a great prosecuting attorney. She didn't hedge bets when she wanted information.

He could easily lie. Doing so had become second nature to him. He could even attempt to protect Peyton's feelings, if she had any left for him, but why? They were the past. He was with her now only to keep her from ending up with a bullet through the back of her head. Wasn't he?

Then what was that kiss about?

He settled his elbows on his thighs and let his hands dangle between his knees as he stared down at the worn carpet and chose to ignore his conscience. Lifting his gaze to hers, he said, "I cared about her. Love?" He shrugged. "I thought I knew what it was. Once."

She winced, and it filled him with a morbid sense of satisfaction. "Any other questions?" he asked sarcastically.

"Just one," she said, crossing her arms. "You stopped running, didn't you?"

"I didn't plan to," he said after a moment. "I hired on as a cook in a truck stop when I ended up in some small town I didn't even know the name of, somewhere between Manhattan and Topeka, Kansas. Beth managed the place at night and waited tables on the graveyard shift. The cook walked out and I was in the right place at the right time. She hired me on the spot without asking a lot of questions I made a habit of evading."

Still leaning against the dresser, Peyton crossed her slim ankles. "You couldn't have used your social security number or they'd have been on you right away. How'd you get around that?"

"I'd give a phony number, then stall for a week or two, saying I lost my wallet and was waiting for a replacement card. By the time they handed me my second paycheck I'd tell them I got my card a couple of days before, but just forgot to bring it with me. I'd promise to have it the next day, but I'd move on to the next town and the next job under another name and fake social. Until Kansas, I never stayed longer than six weeks in any location."

She looked at him thoughtfully. "Why was Kansas different? Because of Beth?"

He pulled in a breath and let it out slowly. Her questions were no less grilling than the ones he tortured himself with every night. Only now he had to face the answers. No more dishonesty. Not if it could cost another person he cared about her life.

"She was part of the reason," he admitted. "That, and I'd been on the run just under two years. I was tired of always looking over my shoulder, and frustrated because after twenty-some months, I was no closer to finding out who the bad guys really were. In all that time, I had zero leads and couldn't come up with a scrap of information that would bring me any closer to clearing my name. I hadn't planned on sticking around long, just enough to make some cash so I could keep moving. Moving and looking."

"But you stayed."

"I stayed. I knew in my gut I shouldn't, but like I said, I was tired and I hadn't had any close scrapes in almost a year. Maybe I'd hoped they'd given up. Besides, if I never surfaced, then their dirty little secrets would be kept. With an assumed identity, marriage would keep me safe for longer than usual. And for a while, it did."

"How long did it last?"

"Almost eight months." Eight months during which he'd foolishly believed he could maybe have a semblance of a normal life, although nothing like what he'd once envisioned for himself. If it meant staying alive, he was more than willing to make a few concessions.

"How long…"

Before the bastards got to her? "We were married four months," he said.

"Did she know?" Peyton asked as she straightened and pushed away from dresser. "Did she know about your...past?"

"No. Not all of it," he said with a shake of his head. "I told her I had some trouble once, but that that life was behind me."

Peyton stopped halfway between the dresser and the faded velour rocking chair in the corner nearest the bathroom. "And she accepted that?" she asked incredulously.

He shot her a meaningful look. "She did. But Beth wasn't the type of woman to take anything at surface value. She knew I wasn't telling her everything, but she trusted me."

And it had cost her her life.

"I'm sorry, Jared," Peyton said, once she removed her briefcase from the chair and sat. Whether she apologized because she hadn't trusted him, or as an offer of sympathy, he couldn't say, so he remained silent and waited for her next question.

She slipped off her pumps and tucked her feet beneath her. "How did they find you?" she asked as she smoothed her hands over her slim navy skirt.

"I'm not really sure. You know what the bureau's computer system is like and what they can access. Nothing is private anymore, I don't care what line the public is fed. You know it and I know it. How else would they have known where to find me?"

"But, Jared, you know how to hide. You were once Navy Intel. Black Ops. Surely you had contacts."

"I didn't have the money for a complete new identity," he said. "Plus, I figured they'd know most of my contacts, so instead of creating a new me without a past that could trigger something in the computer, I crossed the border into Missouri, then hit the big cemetery in Independence in search of a male who'd roughly be around my age if he were still alive. A trip to the county registrar's office for a copy of the birth certificate, then back across the border for a social security number and Kansas driver's license, and Sean Barnett was reincarnated."

"Let me guess. You found someone who'd recently died."

He made a sound that roughly resembled a laugh. "I'm not stupid, Peyton. No, I used the name of a child who died roughly thirty years ago, one who wouldn't have a traceable past. I honestly don't know how they found me, but they did.

"Since Beth and I both worked graveyard at the truck stop, afternoons were free. I'd left her at home and had taken her car in to have the brakes done. Normal everyday stuff. While I was waiting, I spotted a couple of suits coming out of the sheriff's office. I knew they were agents, so I called Beth right away, told her the jig was up and we should meet at the location we'd discussed, about an hour after sunset."

"How much did she know? You had to have told her something, or was she really operating on blind trust?"

He shook his head. "By this time, I'd told her I was wanted by the FBI for crimes I didn't commit. That was good enough for her," he said with a condescending lift of one eyebrow.

Peyton kept silent. A smart move, since she

couldn't very well argue with him when his word hadn't been enough for her, not without him calling her a hypocrite yet again.

"I played it cautious," he continued, "and parked the car in the brush, about a mile and a half away from where we were supposed to meet, then stayed off the road as I made my way down toward the lake. Only about a half mile ahead, the place was crawling with agents. A couple I recognized from the D.C. office, but the rest were probably locals from Kansas City. My first instinct was to double back and get the hell out of there, but I couldn't leave without Beth. I didn't know if she had told them about the house or the lake and they were holding her there, but I know if it'd been me, I'd have taken her to the house, where there was less of a chance of her being injured if anything went down. So that's where I went first. If she wasn't there, then I'd approach the lake from another location and find a way to get us both out of there."

He ran his hand through his hair and released a short, impatient breath. With each memory he dredged up, his guilt mounted. He'd been foolish to believe that keeping Beth in the dark might save her life if they ever did catch up with him.

"By the time I made it back to the house, I knew something was wrong, especially since there wasn't a single agent near the place. I searched the perimeter before going in, then made my way toward the bungalow.

"I went in through the back, and found her in the kitchen. She'd been shot, and the place looked as if we'd had some huge fight."

Peyton gasped. "To make it look like you did it.

But why? And who in the bureau would do such a thing to an innocent woman?''

Restless energy or a vain attempt to escape the guilt had him off the bed and pacing the room again. ''Someone with something to hide. And they want to keep it that way.''

She straightened and wrapped her arms around her middle once more as she leaned forward. ''But why kill Beth?'' she asked. ''If you didn't tell her anything important, what could she possibly know?''

He stopped his pacing and listened, then shook his head in dismissal when he realized it was just the brake of some 18-wheeler coming off the highway. ''Considering we were married, everything, as far as they knew. Or nothing. Obviously Beth was a loose end someone wasn't willing to risk.''

''Do you think it's one person?''

Jared continued his contribution in wearing out the already worn carpet. ''I don't know yet. And until I do know who is pulling the strings, your life, and mine, aren't worth shit.''

''But why me?'' That hint of fear reappeared in her eyes. ''We haven't seen each other since you left. It just doesn't make sense that they'd come after me instead of your sister.''

Peyton was light years away from dim-witted, but she sure as hell was stubborn on the issue of her own safety. ''It makes perfect sense,'' he argued. ''They couldn't get to Dee. And now she has someone who'd give his life to protect her. Plus they already know there's nothing she can tell them. They've tried and they've never been able to get to her. They got to Beth and now they're coming after you for the same reason.''

Peyton shook her head in denial. "You can't know that."

He knelt on the floor beside the bed. "Yes, I can. And they've already started." He lifted the mattress and pulled out the material Chase had given him. "They've been building a case against you from the very beginning."

"Building a case? But I've done nothing wrong," she railed. "There's nothing to build a case with."

He emitted an abrupt bark of laughter as he stood and crossed the room. "Neither have I, and look where I've been the last three years." He handed her the envelope. "I promised you an explanation and here it is. Everything I know so far."

Peyton's insides trembled as she stared at the envelope, afraid to open it. Afraid to see the truth? Maybe. Or maybe her fear stemmed from something much more simple and a whole lot more complex. Such as once she reviewed the documents contained inside, she knew her life would be forever changed. And not necessarily for the better.

Jared leaned against the wall once more. "Take a look, and you'll see for yourself, Peyton. This is a whole lot bigger than even I imagined. It doesn't justify what they did to Beth, but I do understand why they went to such extreme measures."

Each time he said the name of the woman he'd turned to, Peyton's heart ripped just a little more. She didn't think she could claim jealousy as the culprit. Certainly she had no right to feel anything in that regard, but even the knowledge did zilch to stop the ache squeezing her heart.

She was still reeling from the shock that Jared had actually married another woman. A woman he'd felt safe with, one who'd accepted him at face value and loved him despite his alleged criminal past. To Peyton, it only underscored her own lack of faith in him and added to the bitter taste of betrayal already on her tongue.

If she didn't stop thinking of Jared married to another woman, she'd go crazy, no matter how much of a hypocrite it made her. Forcing herself to concentrate on the envelope in her hands, she lifted the flap and pulled the documents from inside. She stared in shock at a bank statement for an account in her name that didn't even belong to her. The account had been opened two months after Jared left, right around the time the feds had finally left her alone. Her gaze skimmed to the balance and she nearly choked at the astronomical figure.

"This isn't mine," she said. "Federal Union handles all of my financial needs. I don't even bank here."

He leaned over her and pointed to the top of the bank statement, which indicated her name on the account, sent to the care of William Minor, a lawyer on Capitol Hill. "According to this, it sure as hell is."

"No," she said, with a shake of her head. "It's wrong. I don't know William Minor. This can't be mine." She tapped the attached copy of the signature card. "This isn't my signature."

"No, but it's close, isn't it?"

She examined the reproduction. "Yes, it's close," she finally said. "Very close."

He crouched beside her and pulled another document from the stack in her hands. "This isn't a coincidence, Peyton. Someone has gone to a lot of trouble to make sure you were linked to the money they claim I made off with when I ran. Someone with a lot of power."

"I admit it doesn't look good, but it'd be easy to prove the money, and the account, for that matter, aren't mine." She tapped the card again. "This is *not* my signature."

He shrugged, as if the obvious was of no consequence whatsoever. "Maybe. A handwriting expert could corroborate your claim, but they'd have their own expert who says that it is, without a doubt, *yours,* and before you know it, you're just one more innocent person behind bars."

She closed her eyes and leaned her head against the back of the chair.

"It gets worse. Look at this."

She let out a sigh and took the documents from Jared, surprised to see the financial records of the Elaine Chandler Foundation and the Biddeford Home for Girls. Dread filled her. She'd been placed in Biddeford when she was twelve. When Peyton was five, her mother had died from complications of pneumonia. With no other living relatives, and no idea of the whereabouts of her father, who took off when she was only a toddler, she'd been shuffled from one bad foster home after another, until her social worker had pulled strings and had her placed in the privately run orphanage for girls. Biddeford had saved her life, and from the day she started her first job, she'd sent a little something to the home every six months. As her salary grew, so did the amount of the donation. But according to the documents in front of her, two donations were recorded as received within a day or two of each other: one from Peyton for the fifteen hundred dollars she always donated semiannually, and the other from an anonymous donor in the sum of fifty thousand dollars, an amount she hadn't made and couldn't afford.

She compared the date of the donations to Biddeford to the bank statement in her name and her heart took a dive. Every six months one-hundred thousand dollars was deposited into ''her'' account. Within about ten days, a check for fifty grand cleared the account, and a donation of the same amount appeared on Biddeford's books.

The documentation for the Elaine Chandler Foundation, the charity that had provided Peyton with a complete scholarship to Georgetown, and where she now held a seat on the board of directors, wasn't quite as incriminating, but the connection was there just the same. At the same time the phony bank account was opened, an anonymous donation of a million bucks had been given to the foundation. The fact that she'd been given a seat on the board around that time would go a long way in building an even stronger case against her, circumstantial evidence or not.

''Who's doing this?'' she asked.

''My guess is someone pretty high up is telling this lawyer, William Minor, to do the dirty work.''

She looked at Jared. The understanding in his gaze was nearly her undoing, and she fought back a sob.

"I wonder if Alan Dershowitz is tak[
ents," she said miserably. "I'm gonn[
criminal-defense attorney in the countr[
this."

A half smile turned up the corner of [
"This isn't the time to kid around, sweetheart."

"You think I'm joking?" She rattled the papers in her hand. "If this information gets out, I'll be ruined, Jared. My career, my...everything. Ruined. All I've done, all I've gone through will mean nothing."

She'd been working in the justice system long enough to have shed her naiveté long ago. Justice didn't always prevail, but for the most part, she still believed in the system. A system that could very well let her down when she needed it the most.

"What am I going to do?" she whispered around the lump clogging her throat. She'd been in rough spots before, some so horrifying she still occasionally woke up screaming from the nightmares. Never had she envisioned her entire life torn to shreds to the point that she could lose everything else important to her.

Jared took the documents from her and tossed them on the table before urging her out of the chair and into his arms. Without an ounce of hesitation she slipped into his warm and oddly comforting embrace. She knew on some level her willingness to be held was in reaction to the horrifying news she'd just learned. If everything Jared had shown her was true, then her life was literally hanging in the balance. What would happen next? When would they make their move? And most important, who the hell were *they?*

His hands slid up and down her back, soothing her

...me small degree. She closed her eyes and ...thed in his masculine scent, wishing this was just another in a long line of nightmares. A horrible dream she'd wake up from when the alarm went off in the early morning hours.

"I promise you, we're going to find out who's behind this and bring them down."

His words brought her wishful thinking crashing to the ground.

She leaned back and looked into his sympathetic eyes. "I don't know how. In the three years you've been on the run, all you've been able to come up with are some bank statements for an account I don't even own."

His lips tightened into a grim line, and her dread became downright despair. She'd seen that look before. Maybe not recently, but every part of him was still firmly imprinted on her memory. She knew in her heart he was going to say something that had the potential to send her into full-blown panic. "Oh, God. What else?"

He turned her toward the table. "Sit here and I'll show you. You're not—" He stiffened abruptly and pulled away from her.

Before she could ask him what was wrong, he lifted his hand and made a slashing motion against his throat, stopping her before she could utter a single word. She listened, but all she heard were the sounds of the city at night. That didn't mean Jared hadn't heard something to put him on alert. A quick glance at her wristwatch told her it was already past eleven o'clock.

Jared quietly moved to the window and used the tip

of his finger to carefully ease the curtain aside. If she hadn't been watching him, she would never have known he'd moved it. He stood so absolutely still she couldn't help wondering if he was even breathing.

As carefully as he'd eased the curtain aside, he shifted it back into place. When he turned to face her, her heart sank. The emotion banked in his expressive eyes told her everything she needed to know. Someone knew where they were.

She had a thousand questions, but he shook his head and placed his finger over his lips. Reminding herself she'd done nothing wrong, that Jared was the fugitive and not her, did nothing to still the rapid cadence of her heart. And for good reason. According to what he'd shown her thus far, she had reason to be afraid. Very afraid.

Without a sound, he picked up all the papers before lifting her briefcase and setting it on the bed. He opened the dual latches with equal silence. After placing the thick envelope and documents inside, he handed her the briefcase, then picked up her shoes, frowned, and motioned for her to put them on before he opened the closet to pull out a packed duffel bag.

Her insides started trembling again. She wished he'd say something and break the horrible silence.

After tucking her purse inside the duffel, he slung the heavy bag over his shoulder and made his way back to the window. The seconds ticked by until he finally slid the curtain into place again.

He walked to where she stood, slipped his hand beneath her hair and urged her forward. "Were you expected somewhere?" he asked in a hushed tone.

Afraid to speak, she shook her head. With Leland

out of town for the weekend and Kellie visiting her
family, no one would be looking for her. Jared really
couldn't have chosen a better time to kidnap her, at
least from a kidnapper's perspective.

"A city cop's checking license plates in the parking
lot." Jared's warm breath fanned her ear. "It could
be nothing, but I don't want to take that chance, do
you?"

He waited until she shook her head before continuing. "We're getting out of here."

Since her voice seemed to stop working, she nodded
in understanding.

"I need you to trust me, Peyton. Can you do that?"

She hesitated, and his grip on her neck tightened.

"You have no choice if you want to stay alive."

She had a flood of unanswered questions, not to
mention all the hurt and betrayal between them, for
them to coexist with unconditional trust.

Would he do his best to keep her alive? Of that she
had little doubt.

But what would it cost her? Or him? She had a
feeling the enormous amount of cash that supposedly
belonged to her wouldn't even begin to cover the
down payment.

With a slight inclination of her head, she managed
a nod that seemed to satisfy him. He snagged her hand
and hauled her toward the bathroom. Inside the tub
and shower combination was a tiny window that
looked barely large enough for a small eight-year-old
child to fit through. With Jared's help, she might make
it, but she couldn't see him crawling through with
those wide shoulders of his.

Outside, she heard the crackle of a police radio.

Fear tripped through her and settled in the pit of her stomach.

Jared swore and walked back into the room, stopping at the door. She followed and waited beside him, holding her breath. The police radio flared to life again, and she was just able to make out the dispatcher's words: "Four David Nine, we have a positive on plate number Ocean Robert Lincoln six nine six nine. Suspect Peyton Madison Douglas should be considered armed and possibly dangerous."

5

ARMED AND DANGEROUS?

Her?

About the only thing she considered dangerous about herself pertained to her state of mind, since she was having one hell of a time digesting all the ludicrous information she'd seen and heard in the last two and a half hours.

Jared squeezed her hand, but she could take no comfort from the gesture. In fact, as far as she was concerned, the blame for those horrifying words could be laid at his door. Armed and dangerous applied to him, not her. Wanted by the very system she'd sworn to uphold was not supposed to include her, only Jared.

Jared, dammit. *Not her!*

With complete silence, he gave her hand a tug and hauled her behind him toward the bathroom. Once inside, he soundlessly closed the door. ''I'll go through first and make sure it's clear. You wait for my signal before following me. We have to go into the alley. There's a used-car lot on the other side, but we'll have to circle around the building. It should give us plenty of places to hide until we can move out.''

Move out? Where? she wondered. *How?* They certainly couldn't take her car, since apparently someone had put an APB out on her and her vehicle. If Jared had other means of transportation, their chances of using it were probably equally slim, since the patrolman might have already checked plates on nearby cars, too.

"Ready?" he asked.

Her answer was a quick nod, because she didn't trust her voice not to sound off like that of a screaming banshee on Halloween night. If she started, she'd never stop.

A surreal sense of detachment fell over her as she watched him set the duffel on the commode, climb into the bathtub and tug open the window. After removing the screen, he tried to hand it to her, but she could only stare at him, unsure what she was supposed to do next. In all her life she'd never dreamed she'd literally be running from the law. She lived within a certain realm of reality, followed the rules no matter what it cost her. Fugitive from justice fell nowhere near the parameters of her life.

"Here."

His harshly spoken whisper snapped her back to the immediacy of their situation. She took the screen and laid it against the outside of the bathtub.

Jared poked his head out the window for a better look into the alley. Apparently he deemed the coast clear, because he hoisted himself up, had his upper body through the window and was pulling his legs through before dropping silently on the other side.

Seconds ticked by like hours as she waited for him to give her *the signal*. She held her breath, listening, but the only sound she heard was the erratic beat of her own heart pounding in her ears like a frantic drum.

What if the cop outside learned she was in the motel

room? What was she supposed to do if he came bursting through the door? Make a dive for the window like the fugitive she wasn't? She had no experience being on the wrong side of the law, and hadn't a clue about proper criminal protocol.

A hysterical laugh bubbled up inside her, but she tamped it down. Proper criminal protocol? She was definitely losing her mind. The stress had just about shoved her over the edge. If she didn't hold on, she'd land with a fatal thud.

Finally, Jared's face appeared in the window. "Hand me the duffel." She jumped at the sound of his whispered words, but hurried to do as he asked. After the bag, she passed him her briefcase, then the window screen, followed by her shoes. She needed to balance herself on the edge of the bathtub and she couldn't very well do that in a pair of high-heeled pumps.

She didn't know which would be worse, breaking her neck or getting caught.

With a deep breath and a desperate shot of courage she didn't even know she possessed, she balanced herself on the tub and reached for the window ledge. Sweat beaded on her upper lip as she concentrated on hoisting herself through the window as Jared had done. It took her three tries before she made it high enough to gain sufficient purchase to pull her upper body through the small opening.

A loud pounding on the door startled her and she nearly lost her balance.

Oh, God. They'd been found.

"Come on," Jared urged. "Twist your hips and I'll bring you down."

The pounding on the door continued. It didn't even come close to competing with the pounding of her heart.

Her arms trembled from the pressure of holding herself in the window opening while she tried to twist her body as Jared had instructed. She'd never been a tomboy as a kid, never climbed a tree, never sneaked out a window to meet a boy and certainly never came in after curfew. She was out of her element and had no choice but to trust Jared.

The truth of her situation hit her hard and she fought down a surge of anger. Trust? Jared Romine was the last man on earth who deserved her trust. He had a history of letting her down. How was she supposed to put her life in his hands and believe that he'd fix everything that had gone so utterly and horribly wrong? Unfortunately, she had no other choice, unless she wanted to slide back inside the bathroom and open the door to the motel room, turning herself over as if she really were the criminal *they* made her out to be.

The pounding on the door stopped. Had they gone away? Or were they forcing the motel manager to let them into the room? Well, she wasn't about to wait around to find out.

Operating on pure adrenaline, she conjured up a burst of strength and did exactly what Jared had told her to do. His hands were on her waist before she completely turned, and he guided her out the window.

As soon as she was on the ground and steady, he had the window closed and the screen back in place while she stepped into her shoes. He bent to retrieve the duffel bag and her briefcase, then went completely still.

Peyton frowned as he reached for her hand and pulled her down beside him. She looked ahead, toward the entrance of the alley, and spotted the headlights of an approaching vehicle.

"Stay low, don't move, and for God's sake, don't make a sound," he ordered quietly.

She wanted to ask him why they didn't try to find a place to hide. They were in an alley, and large trash receptacles and wooden crates were more than plentiful.

Crouched down and pressed against the wall, she felt exposed, even if they were hidden in the shadows. She struggled to keep her breathing even so as to make as little noise as possible. Panic gripped her the second the car turned on a spotlight, telling her without a doubt the cops were indeed looking for them. She had no idea if the officer pounding on the door had entered the motel room, or if the patrolman slowly coming toward them was the same guy. In her mind, what did it matter? Just the fact that she was a wanted woman was enough to have her scared witless.

The definite chill of the fall-night air nipped at her legs, hands and face. The warmth of the sultry Indian summer that had blanketed the area for the past few days had finally passed, leaving her cold and miserable. The patrolman continued to drive slowly in their direction. The spotlight shone somewhere above their heads, probably at waist or shoulder height, she guessed. Moonlight slashed through the alley, but thankfully, because of the angle, didn't reach the pavement or bottom half of the wall where they were crouched.

Another three feet and he'd be directly in front of them.

Two feet.

She tucked her head near Jared's shoulder and started a silent litany of every novena Sister Patricia had taught the girls of the Biddeford Home. The prayers ran together in her mind, one drifting into another at the speed of light.

Twelve inches!

The spotlight flashed above them. Peyton held her breath, waiting for them to be discovered. Her calves burned in pain and trembled from the added pressure caused by the angle of her feet, thanks to her shoes, not to mention the cold making her toes and fingers numb.

The patrolman drove past them without stopping.

The urge to expel a huge sigh of relief overwhelmed her, but she resisted with every ounce of willpower in her arsenal, lest she be heard.

The two of them remained crouched against the wall as the patrolman continued to drive farther down the alley. How long Jared planned for them to stay hidden in the shadows, she hadn't a clue, but she certainly hoped she could shift her feet and at least get the blood flowing through her limbs again soon. She didn't know how much longer she could remain in such an uncomfortable position.

A slash of light above them cut across the alley. Someone was in the bathroom they'd just left. Her grip on Jared's arm tightened. The patrolman searching the alley with his spotlight might not have seen them, thanks to the angle of the moonlight, but if the cops inside opened the window and looked down, they were as sure as caught.

Jared shook his head with the least amount of movement possible, whether trying to convey that he believed everything was going to be all right or to keep her quiet for a little while longer, she couldn't guess. Taking the safest and most comforting route possible, she opted for a dual meaning.

The patrolman stopped in front of a stack of wooden crates, flashing his spotlight over the area and bringing the light down to shine upon the lower section of the wall. At least now she understood why Jared hadn't tried to dive behind the discarded crates.

Not only were her calves still screaming in protest, but the muscles in the back of her thighs began to cramp. She fought hard to ignore the pain, but she didn't know how much longer she could hold out like this. She tried to wiggle her toes in a vain attempt to relieve some pressure, but since they were already numb from the cold, it was of little use.

Who was she kidding? Her physical condition should be the least of her worries. Emotionally, she was a powder keg just waiting for the next spark to set her off.

The light from the bathroom window flicked off at the same time the patrol car resumed its slow crawl to the other end of the alley. After three more stops so the officer could perform another cursory search of a large trash receptacle and more discarded crates and boxes, the patrol car finally left the alley.

Peyton sagged against Jared as she drew large gulps of air into her deprived lungs. Her heart rate was eons away from resuming anything remotely close to normal, and she didn't think for a second she'd ever feel completely safe again.

He shifted his position to slip his arms around her. "You're trembling," he whispered against her ear.

"It sure as hell isn't all from the cold," she replied quietly. "I have one thing to say to you, Jared. You got me into this mess, and you'd damned well better get me out of it."

"I will, Peyton. I promise you."

The sincerity in his words did zilch to return her to her own comfort zone. Jared had let her down once before, when she'd needed him the most. One of these days maybe she'd have the opportunity to tell him about it. Now wasn't the time…not when they were both trying to stay alive.

JARED ROLLED THE VEHICLE to a stop at the corner of the Baltimore residential street and shot Peyton a glance he hoped conveyed how crazy he thought her suggestion. "Are you looking to get caught? Ever hear of a paper trail?"

"Grand theft auto isn't exactly playing it safe," she reminded him with a hefty dose of sarcasm.

He couldn't deny her point, but how else were they supposed to make it out of the city? On foot? Hardly. Helping themselves to a barely used Ford Expedition from the car lot next to the motel didn't exactly qualify as his most brilliant move, but if they could find another black SUV, he'd swap the plates, buying them a little extra time. The number of people who actually looked at their own license plates each morning were few and far between.

Still, hitting the ATM machines for cash would

mean a huge risk. It could take as little as thirty minutes before someone was alerted, if they were monitoring, which he was bloody sure they would be.

He turned left at the corner and headed down another residential street in search of a matching vehicle.

"And I *am* thinking about a paper trail," she said. "I only have something like a hundred and ten bucks in my wallet. What about you?"

"A little over two hundred."

"We can't use my credit cards to support us until we're out of danger *because* they're traceable. But if we go back into D.C., then no one will know which direction we've gone," she argued. "Unless we intentionally lead them in the wrong direction."

Damned if she didn't have a good idea. Provided they were able to even make a withdrawal. "It'll only work if they haven't frozen your assets yet," he told her. "Considering how quickly they had the cops looking for your car, it's entirely possible. Either way, they're going to know you tried to access cash."

She reached over to turn the heater up a notch. "Someone is already trying to make me look guilty. What's the difference? We have nothing to lose by at least trying."

Well, for one thing, their lives, but he didn't feel it necessary to remind her. She'd had more than her fair share of shocking revelations for one night, and there were more to come.

Frankly, he had to give her credit. After everything he'd told her thus far, she appeared to be handling it well. Of course, he'd only touched the tip of the iceberg they were heading for at warp speed. By the time he told her everything, he expected a meltdown on her part, albeit a temporary one. No one could keep Peyton Douglas down for long. Never a weepy type of female, she had an innate sense of survival that would go a hell of a long way in keeping them alive. But only if he could regain her complete trust, because without it, they were as good as dead.

The interior of the vehicle warmed up considerably. A quick glance in her direction told him she was finally starting to relax, if only marginally. The color had come back into her cheeks, and the wild-eyed fright in her gaze had shifted to alert caution. After their close scrape back at the motel, he'd been worried about her, until she'd threatened him.

He made a right at the next corner. "We need somewhere to hole up until we can put everything together. A place as far away from the city as we can get, but still close enough for us to make it back within a day or so."

"Jared," she said with a hint of melancholy in her voice. "I know a place."

He immediately knew where she was referring to, as well. They'd taken their first vacation together there, spending two glorious weeks filled with long walks along the shore, visiting the shops in the village and searching out antiques. They'd made love every chance they'd gotten. He'd known then that she was the one for him. It'd been the first time he'd told her he loved her.

He looked over at her and couldn't help the grin that tugged his mouth. "Maine," he said.

A soft answering smile curved her mouth. She remembered, too.

"I don't think anyone knows about the cottage, so

I doubt there's any way I can be connected, since I don't own it. It could give us time to figure out what we've got to do to make all this ugliness go away.''

"It might work," he agreed. The cottage belonged to Harry Shanks, who had probably retired by now from the Biddeford Home. He'd been in charge of maintenance at Biddeford, and the only father figure Peyton had ever known, or rather, come to trust.

"At the very least it might buy us a couple of extra days," she said.

Okay, so she was right. If they could manage to lead the bastards astray, it just might give them a few extra days to come up with a solid plan to get their lives back. If they made the drive down to Richmond, used one of her credit cards to gas up the vehicle, then shot over to Petersburg to rent a motel room they wouldn't use, it'd look as though they were heading south, down toward Norfolk. Instead, they'd cross Virginia to Roanoke before taking the interior highways north into Maine.

"There!" she said, pointing toward a redbrick home on the right. "A black Expedition."

Jared slowed. Sure enough, parked in the driveway was a matching vehicle. "You're getting good at this."

"Yeah. Too good," she said with a self-deprecating shake of her head. "And that's only one of the things about all this that's scaring me."

Jared circled the block and parked four doors away from the other Expedition. "Climb over into the driver's seat," he told her as he killed the engine. "If anything happens, I want you to drive as fast as you can to get the hell out of here."

Even in the shadows of the interior of [...] he could make out the slight widening of [...]

"Shouldn't we keep the motor running [...]

He unfastened his seat belt. "No. It's [...] night. An idling vehicle this late could draw attention we don't need."

He got out and waited for her to negotiate the console and slide into the driver's seat. Her skirt inched up, revealing slim thighs. The denim of his jeans felt tighter than a wet suit all of a sudden. He pulled in a deep breath and let it out slowly. Now was not the time to be lusting after a woman—especially one who didn't trust him.

He opened the rear passenger door and pulled a screwdriver out of his duffel. "No matter what happens, don't try to be a hero, Peyton. Just drive and get the hell out of here."

"I will," she said, her tone somber.

"Do you understand?"

She sighed impatiently. "Yes, Jared. I understand."

"I want you to go to Cole Harbor, South Carolina. Dee is there. And Chase. He'll know what to do." Jared caught her reflection in the rearview mirror and gave her a stern look. "Promise me, Peyton."

After a moment, she finally nodded, then quickly shifted her attention to the quiet residential area around them. They weren't in a position to hedge bets or tiptoe around the truth, and while he suspected she'd had more reality dumped on her than any sane person should be forced to handle in a matter of a few hours, she was holding up damned well.

He closed the door as quietly as possible, then surveyed the neighborhood before making his way up the

..et to the matching Expedition. In a matter of minutes he had the plates switched without incident, and was heading back toward Peyton.

After securing the new plates on their stolen vehicle, he drove back toward the city. Relatively light traffic had them making good time, and soon he was heading for the financial district of the D.C. area. He parked around the corner from one of the city's largest financial institutions, which housed a dozen ATMs. The area was relatively well lit, and thankfully deserted.

He parked and scanned the street. Satisfied they were alone, he shut down the engine and turned to Peyton.

"Where's my purse?" she asked.

"In my duffel bag."

He moved to unfasten his seat belt, but she beat him to it and climbed onto the seat to reach into the back. While she unzipped his bag and searched for her purse, he couldn't help enjoying the view of her curvy backside pressing enticingly against the navy blue fabric of her skirt. His gaze dipped, following the line down to the exposed skin between her knees and mid-thigh. Damn if a surge of desire didn't go shooting straight through his body to settle with pinpoint accuracy in his cock.

He looked away in a vain attempt to cool the sudden heat of his body. The kiss they'd shared in the motel room had made him hot and achy. He was suffering from residual effects. That was the only logical explanation for his reaction to the delectable view of her very feminine posterior.

They were running for their lives. This was not the

time, nor the place, for him to be conjuring fantasies starring the tempting delights of Peyton's sweet body. He was playing with fire, because he was damned sure it wouldn't take much for him to erupt.

She turned and sat down to riffle through her purse. He expected her to slip her wallet out and retrieve her credit cards, but instead she produced a half-eaten candy bar.

She tore away the wrapper and bit down, closing her eyes and issuing a soft moan that had his body stirring once again. He knew that moan, the one that always indicated to him he'd taken the right path that would lead to her ultimate satisfaction.

"Hungry?" he asked, unbuckling his seat belt, hoping to derail the path his own thoughts had taken.

She nodded and took another bite. "Starved," she said, after she swallowed. "I haven't eaten since lunch." She glanced at her watch. "Over fourteen hours ago."

"Once we're safely out of the city, we'll make a quick stop for a bite to eat, okay?"

She gave him a grateful smile and polished off the remainder of the chocolate bar.

"How many credit cards can we use?"

"Six that have a higher cash-advance limit." She dug in her purse again and found her wallet. "I don't know what the limit is on these ATMs, though. We might only be able to withdraw three or four hundred dollars on each one, and that'd be it for twenty-four hours."

He held out his hand as she started slipping cards from their protective slots. "Give me half. It could save us valuable time."

She stared at him as if he'd grown two heads. "You're coming with me?" she asked, a note of incredulity in her voice. "But you can't. Whoever is looking for me will know we're together."

"That's the point, Peyton. I *want* them to know we're together."

She shook her head. "No! It's bad enough they're looking for me already. You said they're implicating me to draw you out. Those video cameras take pictures every three seconds. If you show your face in front of an ATM, it's game over. You'll be playing right into their hands."

He gave her a grin that held no warmth. "That's what I'm hoping for."

She reached out and laid her hand on his forearm. Her fingers were still chilled, but soft and smooth against his roughened skin. "Jared."

"Listen, Peyton." He slipped his hand over her trembling fingers and squeezed gently. "I figure in about two to three hours at the very most, they're going to know you're with me. That's going to tell whoever is pulling the strings that I'm onto them. It's going to make them extremely nervous when they realize it, too."

"Which means they just might start making mistakes."

"Right you are, sweetheart. Now give me half of those cards and your PIN numbers."

She handed him three cards, then looked away. "They're all the same. Numbers have never been my forte. Five, two, seven, three."

Realization dawned and he understood her need not to look at him. She still had the same number as when they'd been together. If she'd needed cash during the night, he'd been the one to go, because it wasn't safe for a woman alone around an ATM machine after dark. She'd wanted a number she could easily remember. He'd talked her out of using their address or the last four digits of their phone number, so she'd insisted on a variation of his name to correspond with the telephone keypad. Something she'd said she would never forget because he was permanently etched on her heart.

He reached for the door handle, trying not to read too much into that knowledge. "We'll know on the first try if they've managed to freeze your assets already. Try for a grand on each, then work down in two-hundred-dollar increments until the machine starts spitting out money."

"Got it."

"Are you ready?"

She glanced in his direction. "No one is ever ready for something like this."

"We need to work fast. If a transaction takes longer than thirty seconds to clear, cancel it and get back in the truck."

They left the vehicle and headed around the corner to the ATMs. He'd wanted to keep the truck out of the way of the cameras so their adversaries would have no idea how they were traveling. "It'll be all right, Peyton," he said when they reached the machines. "We're going to get out of this."

"I hope you're right," she said, then walked up to the machine and inserted her card.

He took the ATM next to her and slipped the card into the slot. After punching her PIN number on the keypad, he started counting. Within three seconds the transaction screen popped into view. He entered the amount of one thousand dollars, hit Enter and waited again.

Ten seconds.

Fifteen seconds.

Twenty seconds.

A message flashed on the screen, telling him the amount exceeded the ATM transaction limit. Two more attempts and finally the machine began spitting out twenty-dollar bills. In less than five minutes, he'd extracted eighteen hundred dollars. With the couple hundred in his own wallet, that'd give them close to two grand. He'd lived on a whole lot less in recent months. Four grand was going to feel like a luxury.

He tucked the cash, cards and receipts into his hip pocket and turned from the machine. After one step, he stopped. His blood ran cold as he faced down the wrong end of a gun pointed directly at his chest.

6

"SON OF A BITCH!"

At Jared's harshly spoken words, Peyton grabbed the last of the cash withdrawals from the machine and stuffed everything into the pocket of her blazer. She hadn't known what to expect when she turned around. Anything was possible, from a rejected or, worse, frozen credit card, to whoever was after them. The sight of a tall, gangly youth pointing a small caliber pistol at Jared didn't even come close to her expectations.

"Gimme the money," the punk ordered. Despite his cocky, gang-land stance, his hand shook and the gun wobbled dangerously in his scrawny grip.

God, what else can go wrong? She knew better than anyone that life had a tendency to deal her some pretty hard blows, but never had she had to cope with one frightening episode right after the other. Usually her disasters were spaced a respectable distance apart. Her coping skills were definitely getting a major workout tonight.

A cosmic force somewhere in the universe had her number and must be getting its jollies out of pressing the button, over and over again. In less than six hours she'd managed to get herself kidnapped by a fugitive, escape the cops, steal a thirty-plus-thousand-dollar vehicle and now, the crème de la crème—a holdup by a misguided youth, who figured it was easier to flash a weapon than get a job to pay for whatever it was he wanted. Dressed in a ski cap pulled down past his eyebrows, and the requisite oversize, professional-football-team jacket, he looked like some twisted comic's idea of the Smurfs go ghetto.

She had no idea whether the boy knew if she and Jared were together, or if he thought he'd hit pay dirt and was in for a two-for-one bargain robbery.

Fight or flight. She'd had about as much fight for one day as she could handle. Flight suddenly sounded damned reassuring and extremely logical. Especially since there was no way she'd allow some punk kid to get his hands on the only money she and Jared had to see them through their own horrid nightmare.

A short gust of cold autumn wind whipped around her, tossing her hair into her face. She pushed it aside, then spun around to get the hell out of there, hoping to make it around the corner to the truck. She'd figure what to do to rescue Jared once she had some distance between herself and that gun.

No such luck. The kid turned and aimed his weapon directly at her. "Where do you think you're going?" he sneered.

Let the bastard take a shot at her. It'd be the fitting end to a rotten day.

He looked her up and down with a dispassionate gaze that belied the nervous glance he tossed over his shoulder. She had the sudden urge to charge the little creep and knock him on his bony ass.

"Hand it over, lady."

She chanced a quick glance in Jared's direction. He shook his head in warning. A reasonable person would heed that warning. But she was feeling beyond reasonable at the moment. In fact, she was downright angry. It was bad enough she was running for her life; now she had to deal with a twerp with a gun.

"Now," the kid ordered her. His hand shook, the weapon wavering in his grip.

Well, he could forget it. Fight or flight. Fight suddenly sounded a whole lot better, no matter how foolhardy.

"Sorry," she said to the boy with a helpless shrug. "My credit card's maxed out. I didn't get a thing."

"Bullshit," the punk said, still waving the gun at her. "I saw you pull it from the machine."

She shook her head and reached into her pocket. Her fingers skimmed past the cash and landed on a receipt. "This is all I got. You want to see it?" she asked, holding it between her fingers. "Transaction cancelled."

The kid looked at Jared, then back at her, moving the weapon with each shift. Jared kept his eyes on the kid. She prayed he was paying attention, because she was about to hand him a golden opportunity on a silver platter.

"Give it to me," Ghetto Smurf demanded.

Idiot, she thought. Obviously he was stupid enough not to realize that the minute his attention was focused elsewhere, Jared would take him down without even breaking a sweat. She felt sorry for the kid. Almost.

She took a step toward the boy, keeping the receipt between her thumb and index finger. Another cold breeze blew around them and she let the receipt fly away in the wind just as the boy reached for it.

The kid foolishly tried to grab for it.

Before she could blink, Jared nailed him with his body, sending them both sprawling across the pavement. The gun clattered to the ground, and Peyton snagged it. Using both hands, she aimed it at the boy's head. "I've had a really bad day," she said, "and you're starting to piss me off."

The kid swore at her. Jared clocked the punk a good one in the jaw. The boy's head thumped against the pavement.

Sweet dreams, you little creep.

Jared checked the boy's pulse, then stood, convinced their junior assailant would be fine, other than waking up with one monster of a headache for his trouble. "Okay, Rambo," he said in a calm, even tone so as not to startle Peyton. "You can give me the weapon now." He never took chances with someone holding a gun, especially when that someone was as emotionally wrung out as Peyton. If the way her index finger lightly clenched the trigger of the weapon was any indication, he was smart to be more cautious than usual.

She glanced up at him, then down at the unconscious kid before shaking her head. Denial? Or something as simple as her refusal to part with something that gave her a false sense of security?

With her feet braced apart and both hands on the gun, she looked like a pro. Except he knew better. He'd tried numerous times to get her to the shooting range so she'd know how to at least handle a weapon, but had had no luck.

"Come on, Peyton," he urged, and put out his hand.

She shook her head again. ''I think I'd rather keep it, thank you.''

He stepped over the kid and slowly closed the distance between them. ''You don't want to hurt anyone.''

She took a step backward and gave him a look that stated loud and clear she didn't agree with him for a second. ''How do you know that? You don't know me. Not anymore.''

She had a point. He didn't know her any longer. Maybe he never really had. Had they merely coexisted? No, he couldn't buy that. There had been that special connection between them. Once.

''I know you'd never intentionally harm anyone,'' he told her, moving closer still. ''This guy's no longer a threat to you, Peyton. You're safe now.''

She laughed, but the sound held no humor. ''Safe? I don't think I can ever feel safe again.''

''Yes, Peyton. You can. You will. I'm going to make sure of it.'' Not exactly a lie, but definitely a promise he had no right to make, especially since those out to silence him, and now her, held the balance of power in their greedy hands. Everyone knew desperate people took desperate measures. And the people after them certainly qualified.

''Can you really promise me that?''

''Yes.'' He did lie this time. If he was going to keep them alive, and clear both of their names, he needed not only her trust, but her complete and total reliance on him. Without it, they were as good as dead. ''Now give me the gun, sweetheart. Or are you planning to shoot me?''

She let out a sigh, then spun the small weapon in

one hand to grip it by the barrel before extending the handle toward him. "Here. Take it. The last thing I need is an assault with a deadly weapon charge added to my growing list of manufactured crimes."

"Or murder," he said, pocketing the weapon. He took hold of her hand. "We've wasted enough time. Let's get out of here."

"Wait," she said. "What if we added to the confusion?"

"Peyton, we don't have time." The paper trail had already been started. This place could be crawling with feds and other law enforcement in a matter of seconds.

"No. Listen." She stopped and slipped one of her credit cards from her pocket and waved it in front of him. "Why can't we have them chasing their tails for a while?"

"Meaning?" he asked.

"Leave this one here. With him," she added, with an inclination of her head to where the kid was lying, still unconscious. "He won't be able to access the ATMs without my PIN number, but he could use it for purchases."

She was really starting to amaze him. "Peyton, honey," Jared said, taking the card from her, "now you really *are* scaring me." He dropped the credit card beside the kid, where he'd be sure to see it when he came to. "I never realized what devious deliberations existed within that legal-eagle mind of yours."

JUST BECAUSE MOST of the nation worked a nine-to-five, Monday-through-Friday routine didn't mean that the government followed the same regime. In times of national crises or games of political maneuvering, the lights inside the Capitol often burned long after midnight, seven days a week.

Steve arrived at his office precisely at 8:00 a.m. Saturday morning following his daily workout at the health club. He set his double-shot café latte on the coaster at the side of his desk, hung his jacket on the hook behind the door, then reached for the newspapers stacked in his In box just as his cell phone rang.

He answered on the second ring. "Radcliffe." He sat in his soft leather chair, leaned back and propped his feet on the polished edge of his desk.

"Her car's been found."

Steve was instantly alert despite his relaxed pose. A call this early from his contact within the bureau could only mean one thing—the chance of putting a quick, quiet end to a situation about to spiral out of control was at hand. The fact that they'd located Peyton Douglas's vehicle was a good start in that direction. "Where?" he asked.

"The Horton," the contact told him. "A low-rent motel near the expressway."

Steve knew the place. Rooms rented by the hour and a desk clerk who looked the other way, for a price. Whenever the senator had a taste for something low-class and raunchy, the kind of sex even his mistress wouldn't provide, the Horton offered the kind of anonymity necessary in a town where whispered liaisons and scandals were considered appropriate dinner party conversation.

"Any sign of her?" he asked calmly, effectively keeping the alarm rippling along his spine out of his voice. There was no reason for Douglas to frequent such a seedy establishment...unless she'd been informed of her status as a target to draw Romine out into the open.

"Nothing," his informant told him. "The place came up clean on a search of the premises by local law enforcement."

Shit. That was not what Steve wanted to hear. "Do you have reason to believe she's with him?" If Romine had gotten to Douglas before they could, then Steve had all the confirmation he needed that the security breach of a few weeks ago meant Romine was indeed getting closer to the truth.

A long, drawn-out sigh filtered through the phone lines. "There's no way for us to know, Steve. Not without finding solid evidence that will physically place them together. We've had her home in Arlington staked out since midnight, like you asked. There hasn't been a sign of her there, either."

Steve bit back a string of vile curses. "We should fear the worst and assume they're together." How had this happened? He'd wanted Romine exposed, but he'd had a bad feeling since things had gotten out of control in Kansas. Romine had been careless then. He wouldn't be so foolish this time around.

"Start looking for a paper trail on the off chance she's not with Romine."

"Right away. We'll start checking out all of her acquaintances. Could help."

"How long will it take to start tracing her?" Steve asked. His patience was wearing thin. Damn, he shouldn't have to tell people this high up in the bureau how to do their bloody job.

"These things take time, Steve." The thinly veiled patience of his contact slipped, as well.

No wonder, Steve thought. They all had a lot to lose.

"There are proper channels and certain procedures—"

Steve swung his feet to the floor. "What the hell kind of dog and pony show are you running up there?" he barked into the phone. "Screw channels and to hell with procedure. You have the authority. Use it. We've gone to a lot of trouble to set up Douglas because we know she'll lead us to Romine, but we can't very well track her if you can't even scratch your ass without asking for directions."

"Give me six hours. I'll have more to report by then."

"You do it in three. And I want Douglas's picture on every network newscast and in every newspaper from here to California."

He disconnected the call and tossed the cell phone on the desk. He'd come too far for one rogue agent with a score to settle to ruin all their plans. There were millions of dollars at risk, not to mention the careers of some very powerful people.

He needed to exercise patience, a skill he'd cultivated and polished. Patience and care, especially when he was so very close to having everything he'd ever wanted. Romine would be found and silenced. Steve knew his opponent's weaknesses, and taking advantage shouldn't be the headache it'd been for the last three years.

Still, he occasionally had his doubts. Romine had been running for a long time. They were never able to get anything out of his sister, and now she was engaged to one of the bureau's former agents, which made her even more untouchable. Kansas had been a disaster. They couldn't afford any further mistakes. *He* couldn't afford any further mistakes. Romine was a loose end that needed to be tied up. Now, before it was too late.

They were in the middle of a deadly game of chess. All of the pieces were in place, and if he wasn't careful, they'd all find themselves facing checkmate.

Not all of his confidence fled, however. Steve had grown up a fighter, and if there was one thing he'd learned over the years, it was how to win. No matter what it took.

THE RED DIGITS of the clock on the bedside table registered half past one. Peyton lifted her arms above her head and stretched, trying to shake off the last vestiges of sleep. She'd feel more refreshed after a shower and pumping a good gallon of caffeine into her system.

In about five more minutes.

She snuggled back down under the covers and turned onto her side toward the middle of the bed. Running water from the bathroom shower gave her the slight reassurance that she wasn't alone.

She reached out and smoothed her hand over Jared's pillow. The only indication he'd even shared the queen-size bed with her was the indentation his head had made for the last four or five hours. She hadn't so much as quibbled about sleeping in the same bed with him. Strangely enough, once she'd showered and crawled between the cool sheets beside him, she'd fallen sound asleep. Something she hadn't done in years.

Three years, to be exact.

She frowned and tugged his pillow closer, wrapping her arms around it and burying her face in the still-warm softness. Had he been so firmly imprinted on her that even now, after all these months, she'd found an odd sense of comfort in just being near him? Could something as simple as breathing in his rich, masculine scent be enough to offer her a sense of security, just by knowing he was close? Or did the unusual stirring of emotions stem from something else much more basic, such as a need to survive and the knowledge that on some level, Jared would move heaven and earth to make sure she lived through this ugly mess?

She didn't know the answer. Worse, she wasn't sure she wanted to know.

Perhaps she was still in shock, she mused. Under the circumstances, it'd be understandable, and would explain why she'd fallen so easily into finding comfort where she had no business seeking any.

With a sigh of self-disgust she shoved the pillow away and sat up, propping the pillows against the headboard behind her. Such ridiculous notions, she scoffed silently, and reached for the remote control. They were making the best of a bad situation until they could find a way out of the horror. And that was about as ridiculous as she'd allow herself to feel.

Period. End of story.

When Jared had started to feel the effects of being behind the wheel for over eight hours without a wink of sleep in the past twenty-four, she'd suggested they find a place to stop and rest for a few hours. She could've taken over the driving, but she'd felt as exhausted as he'd looked. Jared rarely complained about anything, but when he'd said his eyes had started to feel grainy, that he was hungry and in need of sleep, she'd insisted. They'd both been completely wiped out, and finding a comforting bed in another low-priced motel made the most sense. Survival, plain and simple.

Period. End of story.

By four in the morning, they'd finally left the city, after pulling into the drive-through of an all-night fast-food restaurant. A double cheeseburger, fries and a cold drink later, they used her credit cards to create what they hoped would become a paper-trail decoy to buy them time. After stopping in Richmond for gas, then heading another thirty minutes south to Petersburg so she could register for a motel room they didn't use, they'd turned west, taking the state highways to Roanoke, Virginia. Considering she had no idea how long they'd be on the run, Peyton had convinced Jared that an unscheduled stop at one of those open-all-night discount chain stores was a necessity. Using cash, she'd purchased a few clothing essentials, along with some personal care items and a bag to carry everything. They were back on the road for another three hours before finding a place not too far off the interstate where they could catch some sleep before continuing to the seaside cottage on the Maine coast.

She pressed the button on the remote now and the television came to life. After cruising the channels and finding nothing more interesting than college football, she settled on a cable news station and half listened

to a report of a typhoon encroaching upo
on the other side of the world.

The bathroom door opened and steam bil
the room. She stared as Jared emerged, wea   ... ..u...-
ing but a towel tied around his hips and another
draped over his shoulder as he dried his hair. He reminded her of a Roman warrior who'd just visited a
bathhouse after a long, dusty battle.

Her mouth went dry as if she'd just swallowed all
that dust.

He glanced in her direction and managed a quick
grin as he made his way across the room to his duffel
bag, propped on the dresser next to the television.
"You're awake," he said.

She cleared her throat. "You're naked," she managed to answer, without sounding too strained.

"Technically, not naked." He dug through the bag,
obviously not the least bit concerned that looking at
him was causing her pulse rate to pick up speed.

She continued to stare in utter feminine fascination
as the sculpted terrain of his back rippled and shifted
beneath the smooth surface of his skin. He had indeed
lost weight, making him more lean than she'd origi-
nally thought. His shoulders looked twice as broad as
she remembered, and a dozen times more tempting.
The thought of smoothing her hands over his back,
down to his tapered waist, made her breathing more
than a little irregular.

"Towels don't count."

He chuckled lightly, but otherwise ignored her as
he pulled fresh clothes from his bag.

The tiniest tug of that loosely tied knot and his
towel would be history.

Yeah? And then what?

The possibilities were endless.

She shook her head. Something was definitely wrong with her.

Stress. That was the answer. Stress due to her current situation had her mind barreling down a forbidden path. She was an engaged woman, for crying out loud. Lusting after her...what? Former lover? Kidnapper? Savior? Well, it didn't matter what Jared was to her, besides off-limits. No way was she going to repeat history. Once was more than enough for her lifetime. Not to mention that, when they got their lives back, that would be the end to their...relationship?

Maybe that was her problem. They'd never had closure. Perhaps she was merely feeling the effects of emotional remnants of their former connections. Lord knew they had plenty of baggage. Seeing Jared again, sleeping beside him, watching him move around the room wearing nothing but that towel, which she wished like the devil would loosen and fall, had brought all those old feelings careering to the surface.

As far as excuses or rationalizations went, she liked the sound of that. Put the past to rest and get on with their separate lives. Whatever was once between them—the glue that had once held them together—had weakened and been chipped away.

Of course, to properly lay the past to rest, she'd have to venture back and uncover all those buried emotions, something she was not looking forward to by any stretch of the imagination. Her only consolation was that now was definitely not the time, not when they were running from an unknown enemy.

Some consolation.

She pushed back the covers and scooted off the bed. "I'm going to shower while you dress," she said, carefully keeping her eyes averted from all that glorious, nearly naked male flesh. Needing distance, she snagged her bag off the chair and carried it into the bathroom with her.

Fifteen minutes later she emerged freshly showered and dressed in a pair of supposed prewashed jeans that felt stiffer than heavily starched taffeta, and a soft cream-colored sweater with two wide, dusty-blue stripes on one sleeve. Jared had packed up their meager belongings and was sitting on the edge of the bed with the remote control in his hand, watching a newscaster interview someone about the possibility of a dock-workers strike.

She sat in the chair facing him and pulled on a pair of thick socks, then slipped her feet into her new pair of sneakers. She stood and tested the footwear. Not bad, she thought, for less than twenty bucks.

She double-checked the bathroom to make sure she had everything, then zipped up her bag and set it next to his. "I hope you're hungry," she said, "because I'm starved."

He grabbed her hand and urged her to sit beside him. He didn't bother to look at her or explain, just issued another one of his orders he expected her to follow without question. "Watch the ticker on the bottom of the screen."

The knots that had been in her stomach since she'd unlocked her car less than twenty-four hours ago tightened once again. "What is it?" she asked him, her entire body filling with dread. She read the news ticker as he'd instructed. More information on the typhoon in the Philippines, followed by a blip about the World Series games starting the following week.

Her picture flashed on the screen. "Oh, my God," she whispered. "This can't be real."

Jared slipped his arm over her shoulders and pulled her close. "It's real enough, sweetheart."

The practiced seriousness of the anchorman's voice barely penetrated Peyton's surprise at seeing her photograph being broadcast over the cable news program. She caught phrases such as, "Wanted for questioning," "Material witness," "Use extreme caution" and "Believed connection to an unsolved murder."

The latter phrase spurred clips from the investigation into the deaths of Santiago and Dysert, followed by another clip of Jared, who'd been interviewed after an arrest he instigated a few years ago made headlines and led to a commendation.

"Anyone with information is asked to contact the FBI," the anchorman stated before offering a toll free number.

Jared tucked his finger beneath Peyton's chin and raised her face toward his. "Are you okay?" he asked. Compassion filled his green eyes as he looked down at her. "I know this is rough on you."

She looked at him as if he'd gone crazy. "Okay? I don't think I'll ever be okay again."

"You will, Peyton," he said, then placed a gentle kiss across her lips. "I promise you."

How could she trust him when he'd let her down before? How could she not trust him when he was the only one who believed her not guilty of crimes she didn't commit?

"Let's go," she said suddenly. Needing distance

emotionally and physically, she pulled away from him and stood. She couldn't think straight when he went all sweet and tender on her.

"Have a burning need to get the hell out of Virginia?" he asked. The lightness of his tone didn't fool her. Not with worry clouding his compelling gaze.

She slung her bag over her shoulder and plucked her briefcase from beside the chair. "No, I think it's more like a burning desire to stay alive."

7

SUNNY MACGREGOR became a federal agent for one reason, and one reason only—because she loved to solve complex puzzles. And since she could barely manage to balance her checkbook without getting into trouble, a career using math or science had been out of the question. Since joining the bureau, she'd quickly learned that her skills went beyond basic problem solving.

Most agents dreaded what they called dead work, but she loved stakeouts, surveillance and paper trails. She could read through reams of investigative files on some of the bureau's most wanted criminals like most people read the latest legal thriller. On those rare opportunities when she was allowed to go undercover, she'd discovered she had a knack for that type of work, as well, and could easily slip into any persona required of her to do her job. Her biggest thrill came from being the agent to discover the single shred of evidence, no matter how small or insignificant, that resulted in a bust. Solving a puzzle like that was a high unsurpassed by anything else, in her book.

She pressed the End Call button on the cordless phone and stared at it, not quite sure whether she was dreaming or not. She glanced down at her breakfast, growing cold on the dinette table near the sliding glass door overlooking the small balcony of her miniscule third-floor apartment. The call had been real enough, and shocking.

Receiving work-related calls at home was nothing new or unusual, except this one came directly from Vivien Kent, the bureau's assistant director. That fact alone had sent Sunny's investigative instincts into high alert. Why would AD Kent be calling her at home to give her an assignment? Sunny had been only one of two or three hundred agents who performed intensive background checks on presidential appointees going before the Senate Judicial Committee for approval on several occasions. Those type of assignments always came from her direct supervisor, handed down from his direct supervisor, Gibson Russell. If there was one thing the bureau adhered to, it was the chain of command. So why had Ms. Kent personally contacted Sunny and instructed her to report directly to her? It was downright strange, as far as Sunny was concerned.

But an order was an order, and she'd definitely just gotten hers. The bureau had received word from the Judicial Committee chair, Senator Martin Phipps, that first thing Monday morning, the president would announce the appointment of Theodore James Galloway to fill the opening left on the Supreme Court by the retiring Justice Elliot. Kent had called Sunny at home to give her the assignment of conducting the standard background investigation on the presidential appointee. A normal assignment surrounded by a cloak of mystery.

Sunny could blindly accept her assignment and not think about the whys behind the method, but her parents, from the peace-and-love generation of the sixties, had taught her to question everything. Just how did one question the second in command of the Federal Bureau of Investigation?

With no easy answers to satisfy her natural sense of curiosity, Sunny returned to her poached egg, twelve-grain toast and the cable edition of the mid-morning news.

Maybe it was her attention to detail, she thought. Her superiors often commented on it. She would've made a great lawyer, except the thought of more schooling than absolutely necessary gave her hives. She'd even hoped to avoid further education alto-gether and had joined the Coast Guard for a two-year tour of duty, but once she'd discovered her life's call-ing, the no-college option had been quickly elimi-nated. The best way to satisfy her need for solving puzzles was to become a federal agent, and unfortu-nately, that had required four years of college for a degree in criminal justice with a psychology minor.

She'd really wanted to be a part of the Behavioral Sciences Unit, but as yet, she was still earning her way through fieldwork. Still, what better job for a nat-ural-born problem solver than an FBI profiler?

Although she'd never been the best of students, she'd still put her G.I. Bill to work and struggled through classes, maintaining a barely acceptable grade point average, but enough for her to gain acceptance into the bureau's training program at Quantico.

That's when Sunny had found her stride.

A quasi-reformed tomboy, she'd found joining the bureau the best possible career choice for a girl who liked to get her hands dirty. Besides, where else could a twenty-seven-year-old woman get paid to wear blue jeans to work, not have to spend a small fortune having her straight, shoulder-length blond hair done or her makeup perfectly applied to an only passably pretty face? Oh, sure, her closet contained the requisite blue suits that were the standard uniform for any FBI agent, but thankfully those were reserved for cases that were simply investigative in nature, such as the one AD Kent had just assigned her.

Sunny finished off her toast and was considering indulging in a second slice when the television picture changed. She stopped and stared at the official bureau photograph of former superagent Jared Romine. Although she'd never worked directly with Special Agent Romine, she knew of him, and not just because of his alleged crimes. He'd been one hell of an agent, someone she had looked up to and could only hope to ever be half as good as.

The screen changed again, adding a photograph of a woman Sunny recognized from the few occasions she'd been called to testify in court. Justice Department Counsel Peyton Douglas, and if rumors were to be believed, Romine's former live-in lover.

Her natural curiosity piqued a second time, and Sunny hung on to the reporter's every word. The piece started out with the usual rundown of the murders of Senator Phipps's aide, Roland Santiago, and the bureau's own Special Agent Dysert. Romine was not only their prime suspect, but now it appeared that Ms. Douglas had been implicated in Romine's crimes, as well. Both were wanted for questioning.

Something about the Romine case had always bothered Sunny, but she could never quite put her finger

on the problem. Although she hadn't been assigned
the task of tracking down one of their own, if she'd
been allowed the time, she knew she could figure out
why the case didn't sit right with her. The Romine
case was a puzzle of legendary status.

By the time she finished her breakfast, showered
and prepared to leave for a lazy Saturday afternoon at
her parents' small horse ranch in Virginia, she still
hadn't been able to shake the niggle of doubt the
Romine case was stirring in her mind, or her unease
of being personally handpicked by AD Kent. But
Sunny loved puzzles. As she made her way down
three flights of stairs to the carport, she realized she
now had two to keep her mind occupied.

IN BETWEEN WORRIES and concerns over the events of
the last twenty-four hours, Peyton knew her primary
focus should be centered on her immediate future. As
they made their way from Roanoke into Pittsburgh
early Sunday morning, she couldn't seem to get her
mind off Jared and how sexy he'd looked wearing
only that towel. Hard. Sleek. And way too tempting
for her to find anything remotely close to peace of
mind. Unfortunately, the cute little smile he'd tossed
her way demanded equal attention. And there was no
way she could possibly forget about that sweet, tender
kiss he'd brushed over her lips back in the motel
room.

She definitely had a problem. Those kinds of
thoughts were sure to classify her as a candidate for
the funny farm. She couldn't even say the lights were
on, let alone anyone home.

Avoidance, she thought, and gave a sigh of cautious

relief. That's what all these naughty thoughts were—her mind's way of avoiding the fear threatening to choke her. Like the way she avoided mundane, boring tasks. No difference whatsoever in how she'd rather wade through pounds of investigative reports than dictate page-line summaries from depositions in preparation for trial. Or cleaning toilets, for that matter. Now *there* was a chore she absolutely detested. Ironing underwear would be a hundred times more preferable than scrubbing a toilet, and Lord knew how much she hated ironing.

The only problem was, in avoiding all those little unpleasant chores, she was now living a way of life that was completely foreign to her, one that included twenty-four-hour jeopardy. A life that required complete dependence on her ability to focus and concentrate on events unraveling faster than a kitten who'd discovered a ball of yarn still attached to a sweater in progress.

She needed to do something—move around, take a short walk, anything. The long hours in the Expedition were getting to her. She'd attempted sleep, but other than an hour here and there, real slumber remained elusive. Truth be told, she couldn't close her eyes without revisiting the image of Jared's naked body, that smile or his sweet, tender kiss. Nor could she muster the strength to quash the erupting fantasies. Like what would have happened if she'd gotten out of bed and flicked that towel away from his body.

The possibilities were endless, and would have been oh so satisfying.

She let out another gusty sigh. She didn't have bats in her belfry. Oh, no, Peyton Douglas's belfry housed snow geese. Big ones, with enormous flapping wings that created even more confusion to her already jumbled thoughts.

What she couldn't quite figure out, however, was how all of these illicit thoughts were even possible, not just because of her current situation, but because of her engagement to Leland.

She leaned back against the headrest and attempted to focus her attention on him. He was a good man. A man who deserved better than a fiancée who harbored erotic fantasies about another man.

Leland was driven. Ambitious. Thoughtful and caring. Not to mention understanding, especially of her past with Jared. Leland had admitted he couldn't quite fathom the attraction, considering she and Jared were such opposites.

Since when had love or animal lust ever made sense?

Jared had always been more outgoing, not afraid of anything and always willing to try new things, even if he did tend to keep his emotions in check. In comparison, she tended to analyze a situation to death before acting.

But hadn't that been part of the attraction? she wondered. The fact that they were opposites? It certainly hadn't meant she'd loved him any less. Yes, Jared was exciting. He always had been, while Leland tended to be more like her—analytical, never taking a step without viewing it from all angles. Come to think of it, compared to Leland, she could be considered downright impulsive.

She tried to imagine Leland's smile. All her mind's eye would allow was the sexy tilt of Jared's mouth.

She closed her eyes and attempted to conjure Leland's image. Instead of his perfectly trimmed brown hair and rich brown eyes, she saw Jared's vibrant green gaze filled with heated passion.

In a vain attempt to shake the traitorous thoughts from her mind, she concentrated on Leland's kisses. Her body heated as she relived the wild, erotic kiss she had shared with Jared back in the D.C. motel room.

Her eyes flew open as a horrible thought pricked her conscience. What if Kellie was right? Could she have agreed to marry Leland to avoid a roller coaster of emotion, like she'd once had with Jared? What if she *was* playing it safe by agreeing to become Leland's wife? Could her subconscious be trying to tell her that what she really wanted wasn't beige, after all, but a lifetime of red-hot and sexy?

Sex with Leland wasn't exactly boring, she silently argued on his behalf. Just because he wasn't the experimental type didn't mean he couldn't please her—some of the time. So what if they'd never shared the intense pleasure of oral sex, or something a little more adventurous than making love in a bed? Just because Leland didn't approve of what he termed nontraditional sex didn't mean her marriage was doomed. Nor did it mean Jared's prediction held any merit, either.

Or did it?

Would marriage to Leland have her screaming from boredom, in and out of the bedroom, in less than a year?

Answers that had rolled easily off her tongue twenty-four hours ago suddenly weren't so readily available.

She tried to convince herself that her jumbled thoughts were only a result of the confusion of her current situation. Her world had been turned upside down, emotionally as well as physically. All her silly notions about Jared and the fantasy of flicking away that scrap of terry cloth were nothing more than a product of immense stress. There was absolutely nothing wrong with her relationship with Leland. She was only confused because the uncertainty of her future was tangled up in fear. Especially her *immediate* future.

Maybe, she thought, after pulling in a deep breath that failed to calm her.

Or maybe not.

It was the maybe not that had her worried. When was the last time she'd been anxious to rid Leland of a towel? Come to think of it, she couldn't remember ever having seen him wearing anything more daring than a silk robe during those times when she had stayed the night at his place.

When had she ever allowed her mind to wander into erotic territory with Leland in the starring role of the seduced? She frowned. Or the seducer, for that matter? Her thoughts of Leland, or fantasies, if she could call them that, were so...so practical. They were spun in terms of their future together, not mind-blowing sexual escapades. A weekend house in the country versus the joys of a painter's tarp and baby oil. Dressing for an elegant evening at any one of the many dinner parties he was invited to attend, as opposed to undressing him with her mind for a night of seduction and pleasure. Purchasing something practical, like a lawn mower or microwave oven versus splurging on a Herme's scarf to use as a blindfold for the sole purpose of heightened sexual pleasure.

Beige versus red-hot and sexy.

Oh, God.

Had she learned nothing in the last three years? Had the pain and heartbreak she'd suffered been so traumatic that her subconscious had buried the real Peyton Douglas so deep she no longer recognized her true self? She was no stranger to loss, but when Jared ran, the pain had been horrendous, followed by even more heartache that had run deeper, reaching inside and tearing out more than her heart. Her soul had been ripped to shreds.

Peyton had no intention of repeating history. Not only did she need to regain control of her life, she desperately needed to get a grip on reality. And her reality was Leland and the calm, sedate, predictable life they would lead together. She needed to speak to him. Once she did, she'd be able to shed all these ridiculous notions that were making her doubt her choices. The right choices.

Hearing Leland's voice would reassure and calm her. Once she spoke to him, she'd be able to put everything back into proper perspective. She was only reacting to the intense emotional stress of everything going on around her, colored and confused by her past with Jared, spurred by his abrupt reappearance in her life.

With that thought firmly planted in her mind, she shifted on the seat to face Jared, more to relieve the ache in her bottom from hours of sitting than anything else. "I need to get out of this car," she told him firmly. "Find me a motel room. A rest stop. Something. If I don't move around soon, I'll go nuts.'' She didn't bother to mention she'd already managed to convince herself she'd had to a visit to Crazy.

Next stop, Lunacy.

He glanced quickly in her direction, then returned his attention to the interstate. ''Do you want to drive for a while? We've got at least another twelve hours until we reach Maine.''

''No,'' she stated emphatically. ''I want to see what's on the news, or at least check out the newspapers. They've had almost eight hours to come up with more lies, and I want—no, I *need* to see for myself what's happening.''

What she really needed was to feel as if she had some sort of control. The helplessness and inactivity were getting to her. She didn't bother to mention she planned to call Leland using her cell phone. She had no idea where to find him, but she could at least leave a message on his answering machine, letting him know she was okay and telling him not to believe whatever he might read in the papers or see on television.

Jared glanced her way again and graced her with one of those smiles that had her heart pounding a little bit faster. Just as he'd always done. ''Anything else?''

She had a list for him. Stop smiling at her, which only added to her confusion. Stop looking at her as if he could read her every thought, especially the wicked ones. And dammit, stop taking center stage in her fantasies. He'd been fired from that position a long time ago and there were no openings.

''Yes, as a mater of fact. A hot shower, Chinese takeout, with my very own carton of fried rice that I refuse to share, and sole possession of the remote control.''

"The rice I'll give you. But the remote and hot shower will have to wait until we get to the cottage, sweetheart.''

So much for her firm, no-nonsense talking to, she thought. One sexy grin with an endearment tossed in for good measure and her lips were twitching as she tried, and failed, to hold back a smile of her own. "Considering what you've put me through so far, I'd say you're getting off easy, G-man.''

As they neared the final tollbooth that would take them into Pittsburgh, his expression sobered. Too late, she realized what she'd called him.

"I'm sorry, Jared,'' she said, feeling a stab of guilt at the reference to his former profession. The profession that had been stolen from him? she wondered.

He shrugged and slowed the vehicle behind the line of cars ahead of them. "Don't sweat it.''

"Do you miss it?'' she asked him. Of course he did, she thought. What a stupid question. Jared had been one of the lucky ones who truly loved his job and all that came with it—crappy assignments, dangerous encounters, everything.

Fidelity. Bravery. Integrity.

The bureau's motto was as much a part of him as her own oath to uphold the law was to her.

Oh, my God. The magnitude of her realization struck her hard. Jared could no more be guilty of the crimes they were accused of committing than she was. He'd lived and breathed his job as an agent, been one of the best. She knew him better than most people, understood his beliefs and his prejudices.

Granted, she didn't know many of the details other than what she'd been shown by the agents who'd convinced her she had no choice but to help them bring Jared into custody, but once they were settled at the cottage in Maine, they'd be able to spend time and go over every aspect of the case. She had questions, lots of them, but if she'd learned anything from her years with the Justice Department, it was how to build a rock-solid case. More importantly, she knew how to weaken a defense. All she had to do was find a hole in the evidence, something as small as a vague inequity, and maybe they'd find a way out of this nightmare.

"How would you feel if you suddenly couldn't practice law?" he asked her.

If things didn't improve, and quickly, she suspected she just might end up with firsthand knowledge. "Lost," she answered truthfully. "Like I no longer had a purpose in life."

He eased forward in the line. "Then you have your answer, don't you?"

Yes, she did, and while the bitterness of her betrayal still stung, it only compounded the guilt nudging her because she'd doubted his innocence. It would be her cross to bear, she realized, but at least she had the power to do her part in rectifying the situation. She had paltry control, but a semblance of it was better than floating around in a void with nothing but a sense of helplessness.

She hoped.

"For the sake of argument, let's assume we can clear our names. What happens then, Jared? Do you go back to the bureau and pick up where you left off?

Would you even want to be associated with an organization that's done this to you?"

"You wouldn't think so, but yes, I would." He drummed his fingers on the steering wheel for a moment. "It's not the bureau that's bad, Peyton. There's someone high in the ranks using it for his own ends. Senator Phipps has someone on the inside deep in his pocket. It's my guess he's the one pulling all, or most, of the strings."

She would have once thought such a statement ludicrous, but after what she'd seen, heard and experienced for herself, she'd lost the luxury of naiveté.

The connection to the senator made perfect sense, she realized. Since Jared never talked about his job, she had no idea he'd been investigating Phipps.

"Do you have something more than just circumstantial evidence?" she asked.

"Just a hunch."

She knew him better than that. Besides, people on the lam couldn't afford hunches. That had to be damned certain.

Erring on the side of caution, she decided to wait until they passed through the tollbooth before contradicting him. At each manned booth they'd passed, so far, nothing out of the ordinary had halted their progress, which she took as a good sign. Still, she half expected the cops to come racing after them every time, but the attendants didn't so much as even look at them directly.

Jared pulled up to the booth, rolled down the window and extended the cash toward the attendant.

"I need to see some ID."

Peyton's heart stopped at the attendant's surly demand. This was it. The jig was up. Any second now they would be surrounded by federal agents.

Cool as cotton, Jared reached behind him and pulled his wallet from the back pocket of his jeans. "Is there a problem?"

The short, stout man nodded. "Oh, yeah, there's a problem all right. With all this stepped-up security, we're supposed to do random ID checks. Customers are complaining left and right. Like it's my fault."

"I hear you," Jared said, handing over an Ohio driver's license. "Bureaucracy's a bitch."

The attendant chuckled. "Ain't that the truth? So where you headed?"

"Pittsburgh," Jared lied smoothly.

Peyton held her breath as the guard looked closely at the fake ID, then back at Jared.

After what felt like an eternity, he handed Jared the license and took the fee for the toll. "Enjoy your stay," the attendant said, before waving them through.

Not until they were past the tollbooth and were heading toward the exit ramp did Peyton begin to relax, as much as was possible given the circumstances.

"That was close," she said. "Too close."

"It was bound to happen sooner or later," Jared answered. "We've been lucky so far."

"Yes, well, let's just continue to hope our luck holds, because I don't think I could take another one of those random checks."

Jared glanced quickly in her direction. "What were we talking about?"

She wasn't fooled by his blatant attempt to steer the conversation away from the scare she'd just received.

And like a gullible child, she snapped up the opportunity to change the subject.

"I was about to tell you that I have a hunch, too, and it says you're not being completely honest with me."

"You're right." He kept his attention on the roadway. "There's still a lot you don't know."

Based on their history, a part of her understood his reluctance to share information with her. Like it or not, though, they were in this together. "Then it's time you tell me, Jared. You can't keep me in the dark forever."

He steered the Expedition toward an off-ramp for Boulevard of the Allies before glancing her way again. His eyebrows pulled together in a frown. "I think we'd both be better off if you trusted me and let me do this my way."

She let out a deep breath slowly. There was only one way she knew of that would allow her to formulate at least a semblance of control—face her troubles with her eyes wide open. "You're going to need my help," she said. "I'm going to need to know everything you know, and as much of what they know, as possible. We can't fight if you keep me in the dark."

He didn't answer, but he didn't object, either, as he made a right on Jumonville Street. For once his silence gave her a small shred of hope.

A lot of baggage existed between them. Whether or not, with everything else going on around them, they'd have the energy to wade through the past, she couldn't say. She certainly had no burning desire to venture back into territory filled with heartache, betrayal and a loss so deep she'd carry it with her for the rest of her life. Still, she knew that until they did take that journey—together—trust could never fully exist.

And without it, they were as good as dead.

THE LADIES' ROOM of the minimart in downtown Pittsburgh was a far cry from even the low-cost motel room they'd stayed in the other night, but Peyton was still grateful for the stolen moments of privacy so she could take care of a few pressing matters.

She dried her hands on the scratchy paper towels provided, double-checked the lock on the heavy metal door and dug her cell phone out of her purse. If she was lucky, she had at least ten minutes before Jared returned from the all-night Chinese restaurant across the street, which would give her just enough time to place a call to Kellie and one to Leland.

She understood she was taking a huge risk, since she had no idea if anyone would be monitoring Kellie's and Leland's telephones. But by using her cell phone, the worst she would do was give those looking for them a generalized location. She took comfort in the fact that in a city the size of Pittsburgh, where cell phone users easily numbered in the tens of thousands, if not more, tracking her and Jared could take hours. Precious hours, in which they'd be long gone before anyone had the opportunity to narrow the search to as much as a one-mile radius.

At the very least, she had to reach Kellie to let her know she wouldn't be in the office Monday morning and that someone else had to handle the Howell motion. If the prosecution was a no-show at the hearing, defense's motion would be granted and Howell would walk. Chances were pretty good that Kellie had already heard the news, but Peyton couldn't operate under the assumption that her assistant had seen the news report and automatically assume she'd gone on the run with Jared.

She turned on the cell phone and luckily had a connection, so she dialed Kellie's home number. Her hands trembled and her heart pounded. She hoped Kellie was back from her weekend visit with her family, but when the answering machine picked up on the second ring, that hope was dashed.

Peyton hesitated for a moment, not knowing quite what to say. She couldn't stay on the line for more than a minute in case *they* already had a wiretap on Kellie's line.

"Kel, it's me. You need to find someone to fill in on Howell Monday morning. I can't explain right now, but I'm all right." She paused. "Don't believe everything you hear, okay? I'll try to be in touch later, but no promises."

She disconnected the call and dropped her head against the cool ceramic-tiled wall of the public rest room, willing her hands to stop shaking. Dammit, she shouldn't have called. What if she put Kellie's life in danger? She'd never forgive herself if anything happened to her best friend.

Maybe she shouldn't risk a call to Leland. When he returned from his judges conference tomorrow night, if he couldn't reach her, he might try Kellie. But did she really want to leave that to chance? He was her fiancé, after all. Didn't he deserve to hear directly from her that she was at least relatively safe, under the circumstances? And what about her need to simply hear his voice? To hear the smooth, rich tones that would calm her and let her put everything into its proper perspective?

She checked her watch. Time was running out. Jared would be returning any minute now with their evening meal. The last thing she wanted was to be caught using her cell phone.

She straightened and quickly dialed Leland's number. As she suspected, his answering machine picked up the call, and within seconds she heard his deep voice. A voice she'd hoped would soothe her, but failed miserably.

"Leland, it's me. I can't explain what's going on, but I want you to know I'm safe. For now."

How much he might know at this point was hard to guess, but considering she'd had her picture plastered on the national news, chances were pretty good he suspected that something completely out of the ordinary was going on in her life.

"It's not true, Leland. None of what they're saying is true. You have to believe me, because my word is all I have left at this point."

A loud pounding on the door made her nearly jump across the cramped space. Her nerves were frazzled, no doubt about it.

"Peyton? You in there?"

She breathed a sigh of relief. *Jared.*

"I'll be right out," she called to him. "Just give me a minute."

"Make it a quick one," he ordered impatiently.

He fell silent, but was he listening on the other side? She couldn't be sure, so she turned away from the door and lowered her voice. "I'll try to be in touch," she whispered, "but I don't know if I can call again. I…"

I what? she thought. *Love you?* The words wouldn't come. Not that they'd ever fallen easily from her lips, but now they were so deeply lodged in her throat she nearly choked on them.

With nothing else to say, she whispered, "Good-bye, Leland," and disconnected the call.

She turned off her cell phone, wincing when it beeped, and tucked it in the bottom of her purse before leaving the relative sanctity of the rest room. As she stepped out into the chilly night air, she barely avoided colliding with Jared. From the look in his eyes, it wasn't a stretch to deduce she was facing a very angry man, who had quite possibly overheard her one-sided conversation.

"You want to tell me what the hell you think you're doing?" His voice may have been composed, but the anger flaring to life in his eyes told a whole other story.

She sidestepped him and headed toward the truck. He dogged her heels. "Since I was in the bathroom, I think it'd be obvious."

"Oh, it was obvious all right," he said, opening the door for her. "Obvious that you're trying to get us killed."

"You know as well as I do that the technology for tracking cell phone users to their exact location is a long way from being perfected."

"Perfected, yes. But thanks to your little stunt, they're going to know we're not in Virginia."

Guilt had her looking away to avoid his accusing

gaze as she climbed inside the truck. As much as she hated to admit it, he was right. She'd made a mistake.

A stupid one that could very well cost them their lives, all because she'd been desperate to find comfort where none was to be found. And that had her worried more than the bastards who were after them.

LATE SATURDAY NIGHT, Steve waited in the elegant foyer of the senator's penthouse apartment while the maid announced his arrival. Judging by the hour, he expected the senator and his wife would be enjoying a nightcap, perhaps a cognac or an almond liqueur. Always the perfect hostess, Mrs. Phipps would insist he join them, an invitation he would very graciously decline. He had urgent business with the senator that was bound to give the old man a nasty case of indigestion.

The maid returned and ushered him directly into the study. A single desk lamp dimly lit the masculine room, which smelled of freshly smoked pipe tobacco and worn, comfortable leather. Steve's own apartment, while expensive and professionally decorated, lacked the old-world charm of the senator's domain. One day, Steve planned to have a room just like this one, one filled with leather-bound first editions, commissioned art, expensive but tasteful furnishings and gleaming brass accent pieces. A place where he would sit in wait for his own personal lackey to deliver important news that had the ability to change the course of history.

With a glass of the finest crystal in his hand, the senator sat on the end of the hunter-green leather sofa.

A decanter of top-quality whiskey rested on the mahogany end table. "I take it you have news."

Steve crossed the rich, dark Oriental rug to hand the senator the file containing the latest information. "As we suspected, they're together."

Phipps took the file and tossed it on the sofa without opening it. "This is not what I'd hoped to hear, Radcliffe."

"I know, Senator. Our people are working on it."

Phipps polished off the whiskey in his glass, then poured himself another. "Our *people* aren't doing such a good job. It's been twenty-four hours, Radcliffe. How hard can it be to find a couple of criminals in this town?"

The senator had a point, except Romine and Douglas weren't technically criminals. However, only a handful of people were aware of that minor detail. Expendable people.

"Until an hour ago, the last activity we showed was at a motel in southern Virginia, yesterday morning. The motel has been checked out, but our people came up empty-handed. There's a possibility they never used the room, but only rented it as a decoy."

"I don't pay you for possibilities, Radcliffe. I pay you for certainties."

"I just got word there's been some activity. A handful of select agents are responding as we speak."

"Do they know what to do?"

"But of course, Senator." Steve smiled. "Shoot first and ask questions later."

8

_____

SUNNY DIDN'T MUCH BELIEVE in coincidences. And while she wasn't one to believe in signs, omens or karma, even she had to admit someone had her number as far as strange and unusual occurrences were concerned today.

Not ten minutes after she'd arrived home from a fabulous day at her parents' place, her beeper had sounded. The fact that she'd been called in to work a bust really wasn't all that unusual. Depending upon priority, any available agent could be called to assist if necessary. But the fact that two hours later she was hunkered down in front an old Chevy Malibu next to Gibson Russell, the director of the D.C. office, definitely qualified as an out of the ordinary assignment—her second in the same day. Especially since they were waiting for word to move in on Jared Romine and Peyton Douglas.

She'd been summoned to the office around ten o'clock with five other agents she recognized but had never worked with, to play the hurry-up-and-wait game until Special Agent Russell passed along what information they needed to know, then ordered them to move out. The fact that Gib, as he was known to only the most senior of agents, had accompanied them, also ranked high on her growing list of strange and unusual occurrences.

Crouched in front of the parked car, she balanced on the balls of her feet while using her night-vision binoculars to scan the twelve-room inner-city motel. The heat from the still-warm engine of the Malibu offered some comfort against the brisk autumn night air, but did little to stop the chattering of her teeth.

While she watched the motel rooms for any sign of Romine or Douglas, Gib waited to give the signal for them to move. Two other agents had been sent to rouse the motel manager. With the heavy drapes drawn on all the rooms but one, which was pitch-black, anyway, there was absolutely nothing to be seen.

The sound of rustling leaves drew her attention momentarily, but it was nothing more threatening than Mother Nature teasing them during a tense moment. The two additional agents were stationed at other locations around the motel. Any minute now the first two agents would return with the manager, and then they'd move in on the suspects. Until then, all she could do was wait—and try to keep the chattering of her teeth down to a minimum.

"Cold, MacGregor?" Gib asked her suddenly.

Sunny shivered in response. "Just a little, sir. Too much sun today, I think."

"Such as it is for this time of year." Gib shifted beside her. "We'll be going in first, MacGregor. I want you to focus on Douglas. I'll handle Romine."

"Yes, sir." She had a dozen questions, but considering Gib had already told them they were operating on a need-to-know basis, she figured he wouldn't be

forthright in providing the answers she sought. All she
and the other agents apparently needed to know was
that Douglas and Romine had been tracked to this location. She didn't even know how they'd been
tracked, whether via a paper trail, wiretapping or a
snitch. There was only one thing she was certain of:
by being called in to assist in the Romine matter, she
might actually be able to review the files. She nearly
rubbed her hands together in hopeful anticipation.

She flipped up the collar of her black windbreaker
with the large yellow letters *FBI* emblazoned on the
back. The move did zilch for keeping the cold bite of
air from making her earlobes numb.

"Here they come, sir."

Caldwell, one of the two agents ordered to wake up
the motel manager, appeared. He jogged across the
parking lot, then crouched down as he wound his way
among the parked cars to where she and Gib waited.

"Matthews is with the manager. Douglas is registered in room eight," Agent Caldwell explained.
"Checked in about four hours ago."

Damn, Sunny thought. She'd been hoping they'd be
storming a room on the end of the motel. That way if
things went bad and fire was exchanged, the chances
of an innocent bystander getting in the way were
greatly reduced.

Gib nodded, then spoke into his communication de-
vice. "We're heading into room eight. Be alert and
stay alive."

Sunny pulled her weapon from her shoulder holster,
opened the safety, then slid the bar of the 9 mm back
to be sure the chamber was loaded. She didn't like
this. Not one bit. Whether her unease stemmed from

the fact that she was going in to arrest a fellow, former agent or some other instinct, she couldn't say. She didn't know Gib Russell all that well and had no clue how to read his cool demeanor.

"Ready?" Gib asked her and Caldwell.

They nodded and moved out. She and Caldwell followed Gib across the row of parked cars near the chain-link fence toward the end of the motel. Keeping low, they hurried across the lot to the side of the building. Plastered against the rough-textured wall, they waited for Gib's next signal. He motioned for her to stay close and for Caldwell to bring up the rear.

Slowly making their way along the front of the motel, they inched toward room eight. Gib stood to the right of the door, his weapon aimed toward the sky, clasped firmly in two hands. On his left, Sunny mirrored his movements.

Muffled voices could be heard on the other side. Gib gave her a brisk nod, then rapped his knuckles hard on the door.

Adrenaline rushed through Sunny. This was it. They were going in and God only knew what would happen next.

"Who is it?" called an angry voice from the other side of the door.

"Manager," Gib answered back.

More voices, but Sunny couldn't make out the words.

The rattle of the safety chain followed by the twist of the doorknob was the signal Gib obviously needed before he charged forward. Sunny followed, weapon drawn, sweeping the room. Caldwell came in behind them, blocking the door with his large body.

"What the hell?" one of the four boys in the room shouted. Sunny stared at the three other youths scattered around the motel room, their eyes wider than the Potomac. The boys had shot to their feet when she and Gib had stormed into the room, and now stood with their hands above their heads as if Jesse James were about to grab the Wells Fargo payroll. The scene was nearly laughable, except a quick glance at Gib quickly quashed any humor she might have otherwise found in the situation. He was not pleased.

Without holstering her weapon, Sunny moved deeper into the room to search the bathroom. An exercise in futility, she figured, because she knew there was no way Romine or Douglas were anywhere near this place. For some reason, that gave her a sense of relief.

After a quick search, she walked back into the room. Gib and Caldwell were patting down the teenage boys. Glancing around, she figured local law enforcement would have a field day with these kids. Charging minors in consumption, with a small bag of weed, was definitely not FBI jurisdiction. Well, not on such a low-end scale.

"Ooh, look what I found," Caldwell said, holding a gold card between his fingers. "Care to tell us how you got this?"

Without having to look at the credit card itself, Sunny guessed it belonged to Peyton Douglas. Stolen? Or planted? Considering Romine's expertise, she suspected the latter.

"I don't have to tell you shit," the boy spat defiantly. The other three boys shifted their gazes from one to the other, all of them looking more than a little scared.

"Wrong answer," Caldwell told the boy. "Because unless you can prove to me you're Peyton Douglas, I'd say this is a stolen credit card."

Sunny holstered her weapon as the three remaining agents entered the room. "Definitely a stolen credit card," she said, inclining her head toward the corner and the stack of shopping bags, filled to overflowing, from the local mall. She walked around the room. "That's gonna get you two to five, young man."

She pulled a pen from her pocket and nudged the bag of marijuana with the capped tip. "Oh, now this looks really interesting. How much pot do you think this is, guys? An ounce? Two maybe?"

"Not even," the kid argued.

Gib crossed his arms over his chest and rocked back on his heels. "At least two." A chilling smile curved his usually grim mouth. "Maybe three."

"That's what I thought, sir." Sunny walked toward the telephone sitting on the nightstand and picked up the receiver. "That just might qualify as trafficking. I'll call DEA. They'll want to be in on this one."

"No way," the kid Caldwell held argued. "I ain't sellin' nothin'."

"Then tell us how you happen to be in possession of that credit card," she ordered.

Though he was looking more and more nervous by the second, the boy remained silent.

She shrugged. "Have it your way." She started to punch in the number to access her voice mail at the bureau.

"Just give it up, Jimmy," one of the other boys said. "They got you cold, dude."

The other two boys nodded in agreement.

"Okay. Okay," Jimmy said. "Just put down the phone. I don't wanna go to jail, man."

She set the receiver back on the cradle as Gib grabbed the boy by the front of his pizza-stained T-shirt. "Good choice, Jimmy. Otherwise someone named Bubba would be finding a sweet young thing like yourself *real* attractive for the next two to five."

The kid blanched and Sunny struggled to hide the twitch of her lips. Although empty, Gib's threat practically ensured the kid would have plenty to say. Except she didn't think for a minute the boy might know the whereabouts of Romine and Douglas.

And maybe that was a good thing.

THEY FINALLY REACHED the cottage in Maine early Monday morning. Not much about the place had changed since the last time Jared had been here with Peyton, something he found oddly comforting, he realized. With a strange sense of coming home, an emotion that made him almost as wary as the feel of Peyton's sleeping body beside his during the night, he hefted their bags out of the truck and followed her over the sandy path flanked by railroad ties and up the steps leading to the front door. The vinyl siding was new and the railing surrounding the porch that stretched across the front of the cozy seaside cottage had been repainted. Otherwise, time had virtually stood still. At least it did in the quaint cape town of Maine where Peyton had often come to escape, seeking a little downtime. Her sanctuary, she'd often called it, and he fully understood for the first time what she'd meant.

There was something inherently comforting about finding the key Harry kept under the plastic, urn-shaped planter overflowing with dried-out summer petunias. Just the sense of knowing that once they stepped through the door, they'd be safe, even for a brief period, offered a modicum of comfort in an otherwise terrible nightmare. Safe and able to pull themselves together, to find a way out of the insanity both of their lives had become.

He rolled his shoulders, still stiff from sleeping in the truck while Peyton drove. Before she had a chance to slip the key into the lock, the door to the cottage swung open.

The relief in Harry Shanks's eyes was palpable as the old man immediately pulled Peyton into a tight embrace. "You had me worried sick," he drawled in his heavy Maine accent. "Are you all right?"

Peyton dropped her purse, burst into tears and clung to Harry. The old man inclined his head toward the entrance. Jared took the hint to make himself scarce. Picking up her purse, he walked into the cottage, giving Harry a moment alone with Peyton.

Jared had been waiting for her to have some sort of a meltdown, and it had finally arrived. Her tears did what her words and a few hours of sleep could not, alleviating his irritation with her for putting them in further jeopardy by using her cell phone back in Pittsburgh.

She'd known the risks, yet she'd blatantly chosen to ignore them. All because she'd needed to advise Kellie to find a warm body to cover a hearing on a motion for some jerk who would probably walk, and to let Atwood know she was safe. Surely she had to have realized that Atwood's phone might be tapped. Perhaps even her secretary's. Jared didn't want to believe she'd intentionally been trying to lead the feds to their location. No, the truth of the matter was far more disturbing, and something he couldn't shake.

Had the old green-eyed monster really nipped him hard just because she'd felt compelled to call her fiancé?

Ridiculous.

Was he being unreasonable?

Definitely.

Was he headed right back into dangerous territory where his feelings for Peyton were concerned?

Undoubtedly. And based on his reaction to a telephone call, not to mention the unrealistic stab of jealousy pricking him now that Peyton had turned to someone other than himself for comfort, he needed his head examined. He didn't have time for useless emotions like jealousy or anything remotely resembling lust. Unfortunately, he'd been feeling a major dose of both for the last thirty-six hours.

He set their bags in the corner nearest the hearth in the quaintly furnished living room as Harry and Peyton walked in. Peyton's tears had ebbed somewhat, but she looked twice as exhausted as before they'd pulled into Maine. Even Jared wanted nothing more than to catch up on much needed sleep, but there were details he still had to tell Peyton before he could suggest any such luxury.

She pulled in a deep breath. "Is that coffee?"

Harry gave her shoulder a squeeze and led the way

into the small kitchenette. "With cinnamon, just the way you like it."

Jared followed. "How'd you know we were coming?" he asked Harry.

The older man shrugged his shoulders. "I didn't."

Jared wasn't buying it. Not only did Harry have a full pot of coffee ready, a pound of bacon sat defrosting on the counter next to a glass bowl filled nearly to the brim with shredded potatoes. Jared looked meaningfully at the evidence as he leaned against the tiled counter. "Either you're expecting a small army or you're planning to drive your cholesterol through the roof. Care to try again, Harry?"

The old man let out a sigh. "I didn't know you were coming, but since I saw the news reports yesterday, I suspected. Or rather, hoped."

Jared nodded in understanding. Old Harry Shanks had been rescuing Peyton since she'd first arrived at the Biddeford Home for Girls. It made sense that he would expect her to come to him in her time of need.

Harry and Peyton shared a bond, and were closer than many fathers and daughters. The alliance hadn't always been easy, and had taken years to build solid trust on Peyton's part. After what she'd gone through following her mother's death, Jared couldn't blame her. In fact, he gave her a hell of a lot of credit. He didn't think he'd ever be so trusting, and he hadn't suffered one iota of what she had before she'd arrived at Biddeford.

Peyton poured each of them a cup of steamy, fresh coffee. "You shouldn't be here, Harry. We shouldn't have come here at all, but I didn't know of any other place where we could hide for a few days."

"Bull," Harry told her, taking the mug she offered.

"This is the perfect place for you. No one will look for you here."

"She's right," Jared said. Nowhere was safe, but at least here he didn't think anyone would be looking for them. As far as he was aware, no one other than himself knew of Peyton's close association with Harry. "We won't stay long."

Peyton took a tentative sip of coffee, closed her eyes and groaned with pleasure. "God, this is so good."

Harry grinned and slung his arm over her shoulder. "I know what my girl likes."

She turned and placed a quick kiss on his lined cheek. "Thank you."

Harry's faded blue eyes misted and he turned away. "You can stay here as long as it's safe for you," he offered quietly.

He cleared his throat and rubbed his hands together suddenly, offering up a grin that failed to chase the worry from his gaze. "Let's have some breakfast, and then you can tell me what the hell you've gotten my girl involved in."

"It's not Jared's fault." Peyton set her mug on the counter and gave Harry a stern look. "I'm going to shower and get rid of this road dust. You take it easy on him, Harry."

Stunned into silence, Jared watched her walk out of the kitchen. Not his fault? When had she come to that startling conclusion?

He should be thrilled. Finally, she'd begun to trust him. But he had a more important question. When had her belief in him started to matter to his heart?

PEYTON REFILLED their coffee mugs and carried them into the living room. The shower and a hot, home-cooked meal had done wonders for her disposition. She still could use a solid eight hours of uninterrupted sleep, but that would have to wait until after she learned everything Jared knew about the people who were after them. She'd successfully avoided hearing the rest of the story, but the time had arrived for her to stop hiding from the truth and reclaim her life. Or *their* life?

No, she firmly reminded herself. Her life. Jared's life. The two were separate entities, no longer intertwined. They hadn't been for some time. She'd moved on and was engaged to another man. Obviously Jared had had no trouble moving on, as well, considering his marital status as a widower.

She attempted to shut those thoughts from her mind. Not only did she have no right to feel even a hint of the hurtful emotions that clutched her heart and gave a painful squeeze every time she thought of Jared in the arms of another woman, but jealousy shouldn't even be an issue for her, considering the two-carat diamond on her left hand.

She'd so wanted the phone call she'd placed to Leland to provide her with a sense of comfort. She'd desperately hoped hearing his voice would have grounded her, helped bring her back to reality. Foolishly, she'd believed that's all it would magically take. Instead, she'd been left with a hollow emptiness, which only served to add to the confusion and chaos.

She set the mugs on the rough-hewn pine cocktail table, then took a seat on the far end of the faded plaid sofa. Dressed in black leggings, another of her recently acquired sweaters and a thick pair of socks, she curled up on the end of the couch and pulled her feet beneath her. As Jared explained the events of the last day and a half for Harry's benefit, she paid attention, looking for any scrap of information she may have missed previously.

For a brief moment, she considered the wisdom of passing so much information on to Harry. If he knew too much, his life would be worth as little as hers and Jared's. Based on what Jared had already told her, and what she had seen the other night, she knew what kind of evil these people were capable of, and she couldn't bear the thought of Harry being in harm's way. On the other hand, if anything happened to her, then perhaps Harry would find a way to reveal the truth, thereby clearing her name. Posthumous, of course.

That thought had her clutching a tattered throw pillow to her chest for comfort.

Jared arranged the papers from the manila envelope in three separate piles on the cocktail table as he spoke. The first stack she recognized as the financial documents surrounding her and the charitable contributions made to the Biddeford Home and the Elaine Chandler Foundation. The second and third piles were new.

A deep frown marred Harry's heavily lined face. "Explain to my why someone is going to so much trouble to involve Peyton?"

"To get to me," Jared told him. "They wouldn't have resorted to implicating her in my alleged crimes if I'd been easier to get rid of."

Harry nodded in understanding. "Seeing as they couldn't draw you out, Peyton became a necessary pawn in their deadly game of chess.'' He reached for his mug, then leaned back in the cracked leather recliner. ''Bastards.''

Peyton tossed aside the pillow and reached for her own coffee, hiding a grin behind her mug. Harry had been her personal champion for too many years to count. If there was one constant in her life, it was Harry Shanks. In the days following her arrival at Biddeford, it was Harry who'd befriended the scared, scrawny little girl who'd worked too hard to remain in the background. The other girls had never been intentionally cruel, but after her constant evasions of their attempts to include her in their activities, they had given up and left her alone. Harry hadn't given up on her, and with steady patience, he'd slowly befriended her. With clear hindsight, she understood Harry deserved most of the credit for slowly bringing her out from behind the walls she'd erected to protect herself, teaching her in his own way that trusting someone wasn't as dangerous as she believed. Slowly, she'd begun to trust again, albeit with a great deal of caution.

With her mug cradled in her hands, she looked over at Jared. ''How far up do these…these *lies* reach?'' she asked him. ''You already said you suspected someone high up in the bureau. I'm guessing Senator Phipps, or someone in his office, is also involved, simply because you were investigating the senator at the time. What I haven't been able to figure out, though, is what the two have in common.''

Jared gave her a look that said he was impressed. As far as she was concerned, there was nothing impressive about simple, basic math. One and one always added up to two.

"Until a couple of weeks ago, I didn't know, either. Thanks to the information I received, the answer is now a whole lot clearer."

"Do you know for certain this senator is involved?" Harry asked.

Jared nodded. "That's about all I was certain of until recently." He picked up the second stack of papers. Like a blackjack dealer in Vegas, he spread the documents over the surface of the table. "Take a look at these."

Peyton moved closer for a better view. The scent of Jared teased her senses, reminding her that concentration was a continual work in progress when she was near him.

She peered down at the documents. The first was a computerized copy of a three-month-old article from the *Post* speculating on the unofficial retirement announcement of two U.S. Supreme Court justices. According to the article, formal announcements from Justices Middleton and Elliot were expected shortly after the Court reconvened in October.

"Justice Elliot has already announced his retirement," Peyton told Jared. "Last I heard there was no official word from Justice Middleton. However, there are rumors the president is going to appoint conservatives Ted Galloway and possibly David Boswell to the bench."

Jared gave her a sharp look. "How do you know that?"

"Someone at the DOJ office told me about it last

week. They thought I'd be interested, since I clerked for Galloway when I was a law student.''

"Coincidence?'' Harry picked up the article to read further.

"Possibly,'' Jared said. "But I have my doubts the connection to Peyton has anything to do with it. It's the connection to Phipps that's interesting.''

"Interesting how?'' she asked. So far as she knew, there were no connections between Circuit Court Justice Theodore James Galloway and Senator Martin Phipps.

Jared indicated another article, this one from the *Wall Street Journal,* reporting on a case scheduled to be heard at the federal appeals court level. The case challenged a previous decision by the Supreme Court that allowed HMOs—Health Maintenance Organizations—to continue to pay their physician owners bonuses for keeping down health care costs. The newly filed case would challenge the constitutionality of the high court's previous decision. Provided the Supreme Court even heard the case, in Peyton's opinion, the battle would be an uphill fight under the equal protection clause allegedly violated.

Jared tapped his finger on the article. "If this makes it to the Supreme Court, there could be a reversal of the previous decision.''

"There's no guarantee the Court would even hear the case,'' Peyton argued. Not every case made it before the Supreme Court. There were qualifications to be met before a case could be heard, either in oral argument or through briefs.

"True,'' Jared said. "And it wouldn't, so long as Middleton and Elliot remained on the bench. Unless the new appointees carry the same conservative views, there's a chance the case could be heard, and possibly reversed. If that happens, a substantial cash cow would be cut off.''

Peyton looked up at Jared, and her argument died on her lips. Lines of fatigue bracketed his eyes. They both needed to rest, but Jared looked almost haggard. Her heart went out to him before she could stop it.

She shook her head, whether in denial of her concern for Jared or his argument, she wasn't sure. ''Galloway and Boswell are both conservatives,'' she said, forcing her mind back to the discussion. ''We have a conservative president in office. It'd make sense that he'd appoint them.''

''I thought so, too. But this tells another story.''

Jared handed her a memo. Unlike the other papers he'd shown them, which were relatively new and free of creases, this one was battered and faded.

She stared in utter fascination at the official seal of the president's office at the top of the document. Centered on the page was a list of names of several appellate court justices, many of them liberals, or the oxymoron of political labels, conservative liberals.

''This is an unofficial short list.'' She glanced at Harry, then Jared. ''Where did you get this?''

''I found it the night Dysert and Santiago were murdered. Once I figured out they were after me as their fall guy, I went to Dysert's apartment. He had to know something or he wouldn't have been killed. I found the list and suspected it could be important. I didn't know exactly how much until a few weeks ago.''

Jared stood and paced the small living room, finally coming to a stop in front of the fireplace. He kept his back to her and Harry as he stared down at the logs crackling in the hearth. "I know it's the reason Jack Dysert was killed," he said quietly.

Harry reached for the document in Peyton's hands. "Isn't this list at least three years old?" the old man asked. "Why would it even exist then? There weren't any anticipated vacancies on the bench until this year."

Jared glanced over his shoulder before turning around to face them. "That's true," he told Harry. He propped his foot on the brick hearth and rested his arm on the mantel. "But when a new president takes office, one of the things he does is create a short list for high court replacements in the event they occur during his term in office. Other than his top advisors, no one knows who makes the list, with the exception of the director of the bureau and a small band of hand-picked agents, who are asked to discreetly conduct a background investigation on each individual named on the list. That information is gathered and given to the director, who then provides it to the president. Names are then discarded if there's a chance an appointee wouldn't be confirmed by the Senate Judiciary Committee.

"Once someone on the list is formally announced as an appointee, then the extensive background checks that everyone knows about take place. As many as two or three hundred agents perform various parts of the investigation to create the whole picture. That information is then given to the head of the Senate Judicial Committee for the confirmation hearings. Before the hearings, the head of the committee passes the information on to the other members. During the hearings, any discrepancies are questioned, witnesses called if necessary, and after all evidence and testimony are presented, the committee then affirms or rejects the president's appointment.''

''Okay, wait a minute,'' Peyton interrupted. ''Other than this secret investigation of the people on the short list, you're not telling us anything new.''

Jared grinned, but there was nothing comforting about his expression. ''I was getting to that. What if someone wanted to guarantee a prior decision by the Supreme Court wasn't reversed if it came before the Court again under the guise of a different lawsuit?''

''Basically it'd be the same case with a new argument,'' she replied. ''It would have to bring into question the constitutionality of a prior decision. That's not unusual. Think about how many times *Roe v. Wade* has been challenged since the decision was handed down thirty years ago.''

''Exactly. But what if someone wanted to *guarantee* the new case was never heard?''

''You couldn't.''

''Are you sure?''

''Jared, what are you saying? That someone is trying to set the balance of the Supreme Court? That's ridiculous.''

''That's exactly what he *is* saying,'' Harry said. ''But it still doesn't explain why you two are involved.''

Jared walked back to the table. He picked up another set of documents and handed them to Harry. ''The why is the easy part,'' he said. ''I know their dirty little secret. What they aren't sure of is how much information I have, or what I'm going to do with it. As for Peyton, you said it yourself. She's just a pawn.

"It's no secret that Senator Phipps is a strong supporter of HMOs. He rallies against anything that will even remotely limit their power. We also know the Court ruled in favor of HMOs. Still, there's a case..." Jared riffled through more papers until he came to the face sheet of an appeal. "Here. This matter is before the appellate court now. It's not expected to be heard for another couple of months. If the appellate court upholds the lower court's decision, this is the case that will challenge the earlier Supreme Court decision. If the 'new' bench agrees to hear the case, it could cause a reversal. To ensure that it doesn't make it that far, someone has to *guarantee* that the conservative balance of power in the Court isn't altered."

"You've said that already," Peyton argued. "It looks like it won't be an issue if the rumors of Galloway and Boswell, both conservatives, are true. All it does is bring us back to square one."

"I don't think so." Harry stood and leaned over the table. He gathered all the documents and divvied them up into three stacks. Two of them he placed side by side, the other he placed directly beneath the first stack, forming a large white rectangle with one section missing.

He looked up at them and grinned. "You pull all the pieces together, and your square is missing only one vital piece of information."

Leave it to Harry to simplify even the most complex issue.

He tapped his fingers on the first stack. "We already know what this one means," he said. "This is what tells us they're stepping up their search and have dragged Peyton into this mess to get to you. Why?''

He indicated the second stack to the right. ''Because you know about the president's short list. Now why is that so important?''

He flicked his finger against the bottom stack. ''Because of this case with substantial money to be lost, to the physician owners who receive the bonuses.''

Harry leaned back in the overstuffed chair. ''And what's the one thing all three of those sections have in common?''

''Senator Martin Phipps,'' Jared stated.

''No,'' Peyton said to them. ''Not if the only connection is the list that Jared found in Dysert's apartment.''

Jared shook his head. ''No, sweetheart. He's right. That's pretty good, Harry. You should've been a fed.''

Harry smiled. ''Who heads the Senate Judiciary Committee?'' he asked Peyton.

She thought for a moment. ''Phipps,'' she said. ''But we're still missing something. How could Phipps assure the appointments of Galloway and Boswell? And how did he get his hands on the short list? Why is the Court's decision, or the possible reversal, important to him?''

''The Court's decision affects Phipps personally,'' Jared explained. ''He's been receiving kickbacks from HMOs for a long time now. That's the reason Dysert and I were investigating him. Someone tipped off Phipps, and he had Dysert killed. My guess is Santiago actually pulled the trigger.''

She digested his theory and had a hard time ignoring the logic behind his argument. "Okay," she said, "but who killed Santiago?"

"The same person or persons who provided Phipps with the short list and helped him assure Galloway and Boswell could be appointed to the Court."

Jared reached for the pad of scratch paper on the end table beside the telephone. "The answer to that goes right here." He wrote on the pad and tore off the sheet, placing it in the remaining square.

Peyton's blood ran cold as she read the large block letters printed on the sheet of paper.

FBI.

9

JARED TOSSED THE BUTT of his cigarette into the sand. He considered lighting another just to give him an excuse to remain beneath the twilight sky with his demons for a while longer.

Harry had returned to his home in Biddeford, Maine, a little over two hours ago, promising to keep his eyes and ears open for a sign of anything unusual in the area. Biddeford was a small enough town where an unrecognizable black SUV encroaching upon the area would raise more than a few eyebrows and wag some tongues.

Which left Jared alone with Peyton...again.

Now that he had her in a place where she'd be safe for the time being, he planned to return to D.C. and confront the bastards trying to silence them. His plan, while bold, was far from strategic, but he was out of good ol' American ingenuity at the moment. Keeping them alive remained his number one priority. As long as he continued to run, they'd continue to track him, and now Peyton. One woman had already died because of him. He refused to let them make Peyton their next victim.

The time had come to turn and fight. While the information he had was based primarily on supposition and circumstantial evidence, he sure as hell had a lot more to go on than he'd had in

With a little luck, it'd be enough to

life…and Peyton's.

And then what?

Whenever he'd dared to consider wh...

he'd regained his freedom, he'd envisioned returning
to his former life, picking up where he'd left off.
That'd been pretty naive for the simple reason that life
hadn't stood still. Not only had he changed, but so
had Peyton. Had he really been stupid enough to think
she'd wait for him?

Considering the jealousy he couldn't seem to let go
of, the answer was a resounding yes, dammit. He *had*
expected her to wait for him to come back. He sure
as hell *hadn't* expected her to let another man into her
life, or her bed, no matter how many years Jared had
been gone.

The fact that he was operating under a double standard didn't lessen his hypocritical feelings. Neither did
the fact that she wore another man's ring. As far as
he was concerned, Atwood was nothing more than a
minor obstacle.

From the day Jared had met Peyton, he'd fallen
hard for her. He supposed, in his own twisted reasoning, even he could make sense out of something completely senseless. But that still didn't explain the
clenching in his gut whenever he thought of a future
with Peyton married to another man.

Tired of his own company and questions he didn't
care to answer, he walked back into the cottage. When
he'd stepped outside for a smoke, Peyton had been
washing up the few dishes from their light supper of
canned clam chowder and fresh salad. Now the cot-

was dark, with the exception of the living room, iluminated by the flickering glow of the logs burning in the fireplace.

Peyton was curled up in the overstuffed chair facing the fireplace, staring at the burning logs, deep in thought. Dressed in a pair of blue-and-pink plaid pajama bottoms and a matching pink crop top, she looked as sexy as any siren with seduction on her mind.

He wasn't surprised at his desire. Just watching her walk across a room, wearing anything from the perfect little black dress to a pair of faded, baggy jeans, would have had him springing a raging hard-on in the past. Why should now be any different?

A lot of reasons, he thought. Time, betrayal, the danger of their situation. Still, none of them had the power to lessen the sudden snug fit of his jeans.

He walked toward her and sat on the arm of the chair, slinging his arm over the back. "What are you thinking about?"

She shrugged. "The past. The future."

As he leaned closer, he almost felt as if he were locked in some sort of bizarre time warp. With everything going on, strangely enough, there was no awkwardness between them, as if their being together was as natural as breathing.

Well, almost. There was some unease, but it was the kind sparked by sexual awareness. Sitting beside her, he didn't have a doubt in his mind that the awareness was anything but mutual, based on the nervous glance she cast his way. The same type she'd been shooting in his direction since they'd left Roanoke the day before.

She moistened her lips. The sight of her pink tongue darting out from between her lips sent his testosterone levels sky high.

Worry filled her periwinkle eyes. "Do you think their search for us is going to turn into one of those nationwide manhunts?"

"I wish I had an answer for you." He itched to have the power to set aside her worries, but even he understood and respected his limitations. "It'll depend on how desperate they're feeling. With that formal Supreme Court appointment being announced soon, I have a feeling they're going to try to move heaven and earth to find us."

"But they won't find us here, will they? I mean, how can they?"

He let out a sigh. "It's hard to say, sweetheart. Anything is possible. No one knows about you coming to Harry's, right?"

"No," she said with a shake of her head. "Not even Kellie knows this is where I come when I want to get away for a weekend."

He reached down and lifted her hand, settling it on his thigh while he smoothed his fingers over her silky skin. He came in contact with the sharp edge of Atwood's ring. Irritation slammed into Jared. Irritation? Or jealousy? He knew the answer, and didn't like it one bit. "What about Atwood? Surely you've brought him here."

White-hot jealousy surged through his body at the thought of Peyton with Atwood. Here, in this very cottage where he and Peyton had made love, had once shared an intimacy only lovers so in tune with each other could have. The thought of those images being repeated with another man had his gut twisting, hard.

Ironically, the reminder that she was engaged to another man did zilch to reduce the pain in his jeans. He'd never been into encroaching on another guy's territory, but when it came to Peyton, he had a bad feeling the rules didn't apply. Laying the blame at the feet of unresolved issues wouldn't fly, and he knew it.

She pulled her hand from beneath his. "I've never brought Leland here."

Jared found that as hard to believe as the hope he felt that she was telling him the truth. "How long have you been engaged?"

She cleared her throat and focused her attention on the fireplace. "Three days."

"Three days?" *Impossible.* She couldn't have just gotten engaged. Not with the way she'd been looking at him all day. There was also the issue of that kiss when she'd plastered herself all over him, making it damned hard for him to keep his hands to himself. "You mean to tell me you're *newly* engaged?"

"Sort of." She pulled her legs up and wrapped her arms around them. "It took me a while to accept his proposal."

"How long?" He knew from experience that Peyton was not the type to leap first without knowing what was on the other side.

"About two months."

Two months? A couple of weeks, maybe. But two months to figure out if she wanted to marry the guy? Jared's own ego climbed a notch and he grinned. "Tough decision, huh?"

She let out another sigh. "You know I don't make snap decisions."

"God, Peyton, you always could worry a situation to death." He chuckled and shook his head. "Waiting for you to decide on something is like being nibbled to death by a duck. Slow and agonizing."

She glanced up at him and gave him a scathing look. "Not always," she said as she stood abruptly.

"True." His grin widened when she turned her head to look at him. "When I asked you to marry me it took you less than two seconds to accept."

A barely perceptible shrug lifted her shoulders. "I was a different person then. And there's nothing wrong with needing to be sure I was making the right decision."

She spun around abruptly. "Good night, Jared."

He wasn't about to let her out of his sight, especially not now when he'd been handed such a startling revelation. He followed her into the bedroom.

"Either you love the guy or you don't," he said, flipping on the switch to light the bedside lamp. All bets that she wasn't in love with Atwood were a sure thing, at least in his mind. A thought that had his grin widening. It certainly would explain her reaction when he'd kissed her. In fact, he should have realized it sooner. A woman did not kiss another man the way she'd done if she was in love with someone else. Especially not Peyton.

Her frown deepened as she moved to the side of the bed and tugged down the covers. "I suggest we change the subject before one of us gets angry."

He considered her suggestion, for about two seconds. "So do you?" Maybe he should follow her ad-

vice and let the subject drop, but there was no way
he was letting go of something he considered important. Why he felt that way was a subject he didn't care
to discuss, because doing so would bring up matters
they'd never resolve. In particular, her reasons for
turning him in to the bureau. She had already explained why she'd done it, and while logically he understood her reasoning, emotionally he couldn't get
past playing the part of the injured party.

She pulled off her socks, then scooted beneath the
covers, bringing them up to her waist. "You're not
going to let this rest, are you?" She gave him a level
stare filled with frustration. "I might overanalyze
things, but did anyone ever tell you how relentless you
can be? Or how irritating?"

He circled the bed. "It's all part of my charm."

She issued a very ladylike snort of disgust. "I don't
find you the least bit charming right now, Jared."

"You used to."

"That was...different."

He didn't think so. Especially since she was doing
her best to avoid answering his question. "Are you in
love with Atwood?" The mattress dipped as he sat
beside her. His hip nudged hers, but she shifted to the
side until they were no longer touching.

She pulled the covers, but under his weight, they
refused to budge. "You're being ridiculous." She
sounded miffed. And adorable as hell.

He rolled on top of her and braced his arms on
either side of her hips, trapping her between his body
and the pine headboard. "Am I?" He made the mistake of looking at her mouth just as her tongue moistened her lips again. His erection started to pulse.

"Then why won't you give me a straight answer? never known you to hide from the truth."

"I'm not hiding from anything. The past couple of days have been miserable and I'm exhausted. Would you please leave? And turn off the light on your way out."

He wasn't buying it, and he sure as hell wasn't leaving her alone until he had the answer he longed to hear. Besides, the slight note of panic in her voice gave her away.

"My feelings for Leland are irrelevant," she added.

Jared leaned forward and breathed in her scent. She smelled of soap and arousal. "You're not in love with him." Arrogant or not, he knew in his gut he spoke the truth.

When she didn't deny it, he cupped her cheek in his palm and smoothed his thumb along the satiny softness. Her breath caught. A heartbeat later, she turned her face to press against his hand.

"Don't do this, Jared." Her whispered words were more invitation than rejection. Her hand landed on his chest, but she didn't push him away. Instead, her fingers curled into his shirt.

"Why?" He leaned in and brushed his mouth gently over hers. He slid his hand along her jaw to cup her neck, his fingers gently stroking her skin. "What are you afraid of? That I'm right?"

She shook her head, the silky strands of her damp, honey-blond hair tickling his knuckles. "No," she whispered. "It's just…"

"Just what?" He nibbled her earlobe and she trembled before turning her head to the side. He accepted the invitation, tasting his way down her throat, to the

f her pajama top. With agonizing slowed and kissed her collarbone, teased her
tip of his tongue. He stopped just below
ist that you won't stop me if I do this?''
moan of pleasure when his mouth caught
hers in a hot openmouthed kiss was all the answer he
needed. When she wrapped her arms around his neck
and arched her body into his, his breathing faltered.
The past, along with the dangers of the present,
slipped away faster than his control, which he held on
to by a tenuous thread.

Logic and reason be damned. He had to have her.

He pulled her to him. Her pajama top joined her
socks on the floor before he captured her lips again.
He made love to her mouth with his tongue, dipping
and swirling, teasing and coaxing her to open to him
without reservation.

She showed him none as she clung to him. The heat
of her body seared him through his shirt. He needed
to feel her breasts against his chest, to cup the full
mounds in his hand, to taste and lave her nipples until
she was writhing beneath him as the passion burned
through her body.

He started to remove his shirt, but she pushed his
hands away and did the honors herself. With each delicious brush of her fingers on his skin, his cock pulsed
and throbbed against the restrictive denim of his jeans.
The need to make her his again, to reclaim what right-
fully belonged to him, was too strong to deny or ignore. The truth failed to shock him. He knew the driving need to make love to her made little sense, but he
was beyond caring. Peyton was his. She'd always be
his.

She kissed his chest, her breath warm across his skin. Her fingers explored, her mouth caressed until he thought he'd go insane with wanting her.

Unable to bear her sweet brand of torture another second, he eased her back against the pillows, then held himself above her as he moved his mouth and tongue over the slope of her breasts, taking first one, then the other nipple in his mouth, gently tugging and suckling until she moaned with pleasure deep in her throat. Her hips rocked forward as her body sought the ultimate culmination, but he was nowhere near finished with his sexual exploration of her body. A body he'd craved for too many long and lonely nights.

He shifted and eased down the length of her slender curves, enjoying every inch of her skin with his tongue. He tasted her belly button just above the elastic of her pajama bottoms, then slowly pushed the fabric over her hips and down her legs.

Ever so gently, he pressed her thighs open before placing her legs over his shoulders. The musky scent of her femininity rose in the air around him. He knew from experience she'd taste as sweet as fresh cream, and she'd come hard in his mouth as he coaxed and teased an orgasm from her.

"Jared." Her whispered plea ripped through him and settled right in his groin, making his erection blissfully painful.

"I know, baby. I know." He wasn't about to rush this, not when it'd been three long years since he'd experienced her desire. Since he'd heard her moans of pleasure and her fierce cries of release.

Using the fingers of both hands, he opened the moist folds, exposing the very heart of her to him. In the soft light from the bedside lamp, her skin glistened. The need to taste her, to slip his tongue inside in an erotic simulation of making love, gripped him hard. But Peyton liked it slow and hot. A buildup of pleasure that would have her begging him to take her, would have the heat pouring from her body in a generous gift of delicious surrender. A gift that would be his to treasure.

Using a finger from each hand, he slipped them into her hot core, moving them alternately inside her, reaching, teasing, and massaging deep within her body. She opened her thighs wider, giving herself to him completely. Her hands gripped the soft flannel sheets, and he watched as she flung her head back against the pillows, her mouth parted and her eyes closed. The image of her mouth slipping around the head of his cock teased him. The imagined feel of her tongue and throat as she suckled him and pulled him in deep, the glide of her lips easing down the length of him until he came in a rush that would be pure perfection, heated his blood.

He tasted the wild, heady flavor of her desire again, gently probing, licking and driving her to the brink of ultimate fulfillment. She cried out in pleasure when he lightly grazed his teeth over her swollen clitoris, her hips arching as she reached for him and silently begged for more. Slipping another finger inside her, he urged her to ride his hand while his tongue teased and probed. His mouth slipped over that swollen flesh and he sucked hard, bringing her more pleasure. Her body bowed, and she cried his name on the crest of a wave of desire that had her trembling.

The sweet agony of his own need for release tore

through him, but he held back while pushing her harder over the edge, into another orgasm that had her calling his name over and over again. Gentle aftershocks wracked her body while her moist center contracted around his fingers. Carefully, he carried her back to earth, kissing the sweat dampened skin of her tummy, her thighs, his hands gently massaging her hips until their breathing returned to a somewhat normal state.

He placed a kiss above the line of her curls. Instead of soft skin, he felt a tiny ridge. On closer inspection, he found a scar, about six inches in length, ropelike and thin, marring the perfection of her flesh. She stiffened when he traced his finger along the length of the scar.

''What happened?'' he asked.

He looked up in time to see her bite her lip and turn away. The clenching of his stomach had nothing to do with desire, but the heavy weight of dread. An appendectomy scar wouldn't cause that kind of reaction.

''Sweetheart?'' He moved to sit on the bed beside her, but she moved away from him as if she couldn't stand to be near him. A chill gripped his heart. ''How'd you get the scar?''

She shot off the bed, found the bottoms of her pajamas, then quickly pulled on her top. Her gaze caught and held his a fraction too long for her to hide the sudden moisture making her eyes glisten.

She looked up at the ceiling, rapidly blinking against the tears, then back at him. He sat on the edge of the bed wearing only his jeans, waiting, his heart pounding.

"It's from an emergency cesarean section." Her voice cracked as she held back a sob. "About six months after you disappeared."

10

PAIN AND LOSS WERE NOT new emotions to Jared. Neither was the desire to stay alive. He'd experienced them all throughout his life, several times over. When he was eighteen, the death of his parents had left him to raise his sixteen-year-old sister alone, using his wits to keep a roof over their heads and food in their bellies. He'd felt the loneliness of the long years of separation from his sister during his stint in the navy, followed by the long hours and deep-cover assignments of his job with the bureau. During the months he'd been on the run, he'd discovered the heartache of leaving behind yet another person he loved. There was the grief and guilt that plagued him over Beth's murder. Yet as difficult as his life had been, nothing could have prepared him for the tearing of his soul upon hearing Peyton's words.

Images clouded his mind as the dark side of his imagination took hold. He shook his head, as if such an innocuous action alone held the power for him to deny the truth or clear the visions crowding his mind. There was only one truth—Peyton had been pregnant when their world had been ripped out from under them.

Had she lost the child, or given it up for adoption? Automatically, he assumed the former. With Peyton's history, he didn't believe for a second she'd be able to allow another person to raise her child. Even if he had given her cause to hate him with every cell in her body, she'd never give a child up for adoption.

Still, he'd been to her home. There were no signs a child lived with her. There'd been no car seat in her car. No small toys left behind in the back seat or cluttering the yard. Nothing.

Which could only mean...

He looked up at her. The pain in his own heart was mirrored in her blue eyes. He had the answer. "What happened?" he asked, but he knew. God, he knew, and for the first time in his life, he didn't think he'd be able to stop the emotions from drowning him completely.

"My pregnancy was difficult. I went into premature labor, but they couldn't stop the contractions. When the baby started to show signs of distress, they performed an emergency C-section." Her breath hitched and her eyes shone with tears. "He only survived two days."

The ache in Jared's chest grew to epic proportions, making breathing difficult. His mind wouldn't allow him to close the door against the anguish. He'd been raised to suffer in silence, so shutting out the feelings ripping through his heart should have been as easy as breathing. Being the son of the great neurosurgeon David Romine and self-help guru Ellen Romine had taught him never to make a scene or allow anyone to see weakness. The lessons were second nature to him. So why was keeping them in check now so damned difficult?

He and Peyton had created a child, conceived from

the love they'd once held for each other. The most beautiful of life's gifts, but it had been tragically taken away from them. He didn't believe in divine punishment or any other mystical force with the power to alter lives, but for the first time he couldn't help wondering if he was receiving payback for his sins.

God, hadn't he suffered enough? Hadn't they all suffered enough?

"This isn't how I imagined telling you about our son." With the heel of her hand, she wiped away the tears pooling in her eyes.

She could've lied to him, and for the flash of an instant, he almost wished she had, saving them both the heartache of a past they were powerless to change. Considering what they'd just done, and knowing Peyton as he did, he guessed she figured her own sins were piling up, and didn't relish the idea of adding to them by lying about something so important.

"When were you going to tell me?" The method of discovery didn't leave him feeling angry, or even hurt. It wasn't as though she'd tried to hide it from him. However, his chest felt as if a fifty-ton weight rested on it. He felt terrible that she'd had to suffer through it alone. Pregnancy. Birth. The painful loss of their son.

The vision of a tiny infant fighting for his life only added to Jared's already insurmountable guilt. Nothing could change the fact that he hadn't been there. Logically, he understood his presence would not have altered the outcome. Emotionally, he had other ideas, and he blamed the bastards that had kept him running for his life. He blamed them, and dammit, he would make them pay.

"When the timing was right." She walked to the bed and sat beside him, lifting his hand and cradling it in her smaller, delicate one. "I'm sorry you found out this way. I know it has to be a shock."

True, she'd dealt him a harsh blow. She'd had time to come to terms with the loss, and while losing a child was something he doubted any mother ever fully recovered from, for him the wound was fresh and raw.

He looked down at their joined hands. Had she ever been able to hold their son? he wondered miserably. Had he at least known his mother's gentle touch as he struggled to hold on to life? "I don't know if the timing would ever be right to hear news like this."

"When you left, I didn't even know I was pregnant." She let out a quick puff of breath that did little to stop the tears from welling up in her eyes again. "Even when all the signs were there, I still didn't realize I was going to have a baby. Maybe it was denial," she said with a shrug. "I don't know, but I convinced myself the fatigue I was feeling was from the strain of being hounded by the men looking for you."

Neither her voice nor her eyes held an ounce of accusation, but Jared still looked away. Romines didn't fall apart. They held it together, no matter what.

"Even my job was at risk for a while because of my involvement with you, which only added more stress," she continued. "I think I was too wrapped up in fearing for your safety one minute, then being furious that you would turn your back on the very laws you were sworn to uphold. I'd never been particularly regular anyway, so I didn't even notice that sign. Once I figured out something wasn't right, I had my suspicions confirmed. By then it had been just over two months since you'd left, and I was about twelve weeks pregnant.''

He lifted his head and looked at her. ''I had no idea, Peyton. I'm sorry.''

Sorry for what? his conscience taunted him. Sorry that he hadn't been there? Or sorry that he'd gotten her pregnant? If their lives hadn't been torn to shreds, would he have apologized when she'd told him she was pregnant? Or would he have celebrated the gift of life they'd created?

He didn't know the answer. He simply had no idea what his reaction would have been to news of impending fatherhood.

She gave him a teary-eyed smile. ''Would it have made a difference if you'd known, Jared?''

He steadily held her gaze. She always did ask the tough questions. ''I regret that I wasn't there for you, sweetheart, but I can't regret the reasons why. Phipps and someone in the bureau have reasons to see me dead. If I'd stayed, I would have endangered your life, and the life of our baby.''

The slight nod of her head told him she accepted his reply for what it was, the only truth he knew. He imagined she had her own version, but he didn't think it would differ too greatly from his. Because no matter how many times either of them mentally replayed the night he'd left, even if he *had* known she was pregnant the ending would've remained the same—with him running for his life and her left to raise their child alone.

''I've told myself over and over again that even if the circumstances had been different, it wouldn't have changed anything, but I still have moments when I get angry.''

She didn't have to say angry at whom. Her pulling her hand from his told him more than she probably realized.

''I don't think there's anything anyone could've done to prevent what happened,'' she continued. ''I've replayed those days a thousand times in my mind. Each and every time I always come back to the same answer. Things happen for reasons we don't understand, and all we can do is accept them and move on with our lives.''

She could've been quoting chapter and verse from one of his mother's books, which had flooded the market during the self-improvement rage a decade or two ago. Part of him resented Peyton's easily spouted philosophical explanation for events that made no sense, while the rest of him understood the truth behind the cliché.

He scooped up his shirt when he stood, then shrugged into it, not bothering with the buttons. ''You make it sound easy,'' he said, more abruptly than he'd intended.

From the widening of her eyes, he guessed the sharpness of his tone took her by surprise. She had to understand the myriad emotions flowing through him. There probably weren't many that she hadn't experienced herself in coming to terms with the past. Losing a child was a wound that would never completely heal. The slightest bump caused it to open and bleed again.

''No. Never,'' she said.

He looked down at her and frowned. "You said *him*. Did he have a name?"

"Adam."

Jared didn't say anything, just turned and walked toward the door to the bathroom, where he stopped and turned around. "Adam *Douglas?*" Why it was important to him, he couldn't say, but dammit, it was. They had enough problems without him tossing male territoriality into the mix, but so be it.

He lifted his arm and rested it above his head on the doorjamb as he looked at her, waiting for an answer.

She no doubt saw where this was going, based on her long, drawn-out sigh. "I don't think this has anything to do with the name on Adam's birth certificate."

He frowned. "Are you going to answer my question or not?"

"Yes, his last name was Douglas." She crossed her arms and gave Jared a level stare. "I couldn't list you on the birth certificate because we weren't married and you weren't around to sign the paternity documents."

The accusation in her tone taunted him. "Is that your problem? That I wasn't around?"

"My problem?" Her eyes flashed with irritation. "I don't think so, Jared. Your being around was *not* something I'd ever been accustomed to for any great length of time. And I'm not talking about recently, either."

"What *are* you talking about? I seem to remember that I was always there for you."

She laughed, the sound cold and brittle. "Physically, maybe, but not emotionally."

He straightened. "That's bull."

"Whenever things got the least bit sticky, you withdrew. You always have. God, you're doing it now." She came off the bed and crossed the room toward him. "Instead of talking about what's really bothering you, you're picking a fight over a nonissue. I see that much hasn't changed. Does emotionally unavailable have a familiar ring to it, Jared?"

He crossed his arms and braced his feet apart. "That's your label, sweetheart. Not mine. Does the path of least resistance sound familiar to you?"

Her eyes narrowed. "Guess that made us the perfect match then, didn't it?"

"I guess it did," he snapped.

"What more could you ask for? I don't like to feel too much, and you don't want to feel anything. I could always tell what you were thinking, just by looking in your eyes. And I always knew the second you withdrew from me. Whenever I wanted something emotional from you, you were gone."

He struggled to keep his anger in check, but felt control slipping away from him. The thought of walking out entered his mind. *Yeah, that's the ticket. Prove to her she's right.*

When he said nothing, she lifted her hand and started using her fingers to tick off his crimes. "When I missed out on my first promotion. When I lost my first big case. Or when I received word that Sister Margaret had passed away. God, Jared. You wouldn't even attend her funeral with me, and you knew how important she was to me."

He clenched his hands into fists at his sides. "I had to work."

She turned her back on him and bent to scoop up her socks. ''I always thought it fascinating how a long-term assignment usually came your way at precise times like that.'' She sat on the edge of the bed and tugged the heavy wool over her feet. ''Then you'd disappear and I wouldn't hear from you for weeks.''

''It was my job,'' he muttered angrily.

''It was your escape.''

The accusation was impossible to deny. Instead of admitting the truth to her, he went on the offensive. ''You're a fine one to talk about escape. What do you think accepting Atwood's proposal is?''

She stood and glared at him for the length of a dozen heartbeats. ''Moving on,'' she said, then stalked out of the bedroom.

He relaxed his hands, then clenched them, over and over again as he counted to ten, twice. He should let her go. Should stay where he was, take a hot shower, try to relax. At the very least, keep some necessary space between them.

He did none of those. Instead he went in search of her.

He found her in the kitchen, setting a mug in the microwave oven.

''I think you're using Atwood to *hide* from life. He doesn't ask much of you, does he?''

Silence. Not even an angry expression tossed in his direction. She moved to the cabinet and withdrew a carton of instant cappuccino.

Jared stepped into the room. ''You don't love him, Peyton. If you did, then what we did in that bedroom tonight never would've happened.''

She retrieved a packet, then carefully returned the

carton to the cabinet. Still she said nothing. Because he spoke the truth? Or because she wasn't ready to face it?

He narrowed the distance between them. "Would it, sweetheart?" he asked her quietly.

She braced her slender hands on the edge of the counter. The diamond ring on her finger glistened and sparkled beneath the overhead lighting.

"If that ring meant half of what you wanted it to mean, you never would have given yourself to me the way you did."

"Stop it, Jared."

"He doesn't make you feel too much. That way you don't lose control. You can protect your sacred little world and never let anyone that threatens you inside."

She flinched when the microwave beeped, signaling the end of the warming cycle, but she didn't move away. Jared pressed closer, but not close enough to touch her. Yet.

"No one can make you feel the things I make you feel. No one ever could, and no man ever will again. You know it. And it scares the hell out of you."

"Don't." The single word was a whispered plea he chose to ignore.

He reached out and smoothed his hand down her cheek. "Don't what, baby? Don't make you cry out like you did earlier? Or don't make you beg me for more?"

"Jared, please."

He slid his fingers beneath her hair and cupped the back of her neck in his palm. Using his thumb, he gently rubbed the tender skin below her ear. "Umm,

I'd like nothing more than to please you. Again. And again. And again.''

He could've sworn she trembled, but as he looked down into her eyes, he was convinced otherwise. Anger had them flaring as she glared at him.

''And then what, Jared? We live happily ever after?'' She stepped away from him and retrieved her cup from the microwave. ''Buy a house in the suburbs, put up a white picket fence and hang lace curtains in the kitchen? I know. We can snap our fingers and the past will magically disappear.''

She dumped the contents of the packet into the mug of steaming water and stirred. ''I'm going to bed. Alone. There are linens in the bathroom closet. I'm sure you'll find the sofa comfortable.''

He watched her walk away from him—again. What he really wanted to do was to follow her and prove he was right about Atwood and her feelings for the creep. For now Jared let her go. But he knew he wouldn't have to wait long.

STEVE PACED THE LENGTH of his living room, turned, and repeated the process. His mind worked better when he moved. Considering the news he'd learned today, he should be out jogging, even if it was nearing 11:00 p.m.

Time was running out. With the computer breach of a few weeks ago, he knew without a doubt Romine was getting closer to the truth. He could feel it. If they didn't find the bastard before he found them, there would be hell to pay...and a number of careers ruined for a lot of important people, his included. And that was something he refused to allow to happen.

He stopped pacing and took a deep breath. He never panicked, but he sure as hell was close to panic now. There had been nothing but one false lead after another, and now, no one knew where Romine and Douglas were hiding.

"Shit!" He started to pace again.

Thanks to the incompetents working for the senator, their position was now more precarious than ever. Romine had cash. Not a lot, according to the ATM records Steve had been given last night, but enough that a resourceful guy with skills like Romine's could literally hide out for months and not be found. The bastard had even led them on a merry chase. First into Virginia, then back into D.C. to a dump of a motel. Steve had been so sure they would've had Romine by now, but instead of finding the lovers holed up in a cheap motel, the bureau guys had come up with nothing but a punk kid and one of Douglas's credit cards.

To make matters worse, the senator had not been happy. Not that Steve could blame him, considering they were all looking at very long prison sentences if they didn't ensure Romine's silence.

Tomorrow morning the president would announce the first of two new appointments to the U.S. Supreme Court. Steve had done his job well, thanks to his connection in the bureau, who had made sure each of the other candidates on the short list had been effectively eliminated. Of that much he was certain. The players, with the exception of Romine and Douglas, were all in place and ready to move forward. Once Galloway and Boswell were secured on the bench, the senator would continue to line his pockets with kickback money from several HMOs, with funds trickling down to those who helped seat the newly appointed justices. No one, other than the players paid handsomely for their participation, would know that Senator Martin Phipps was responsible for maintaining the balance of the United States Supreme Court to ensure further riches in the biggest moneymaking scam since Whitewater.

Implicating Douglas had brought Romine out of hiding, but only long enough to take the little lady on the lam with him. That had been a twist Steve hadn't anticipated. The plan had been to draw Douglas into the quagmire, then wait for Romine to show up like a knight on a white charger to save his damsel in distress. Except Romine had somehow known their plan. As usual, he'd been two steps ahead of them. Someone had helped the bastard. Steve suspected the last agent on the case, but he had no proof. Yet.

He stopped pacing and dropped onto the sofa. Leaning back, he propped his fingertips together and tapped them rhythmically against his lips. What if they sent someone to talk to the last agent to work the Romine files? Would it make a difference? Could it bring them closer to silencing Romine?

Possibly.

Steve reached for his cell phone and dialed. Whoever was sent to question the last agent on the Romine case needed to be expendable. They couldn't run the risk of acquiring another wild card.

Not a problem, he thought as he waited for the call to connect. He'd even take care of it himself, after he had the information he needed, because it wouldn't be the first time he'd gotten blood on his hands.

11

AFTER TWO HOURS of tossing and turning, Peyton gave up trying to sleep. She'd thought getting up and walking around might help, at least in terms of tiring herself out, but the floorboards creaked. In the middle of the night, the sound had all the subtlety of a wrecking ball crashing into a brick building. The last thing she wanted was for Jared to know she was still awake. Being Jared, he'd probably suspect the motivation behind her nocturnal activities—that she couldn't stop thinking about him or their conversation.

She kept her gaze on the white glow of the sandy beach under the moonlight outside the bedroom window, while absently spinning the diamond engagement ring around on her finger. If there was one thing she really hated, it was when Jared was right. Right? she wondered. Or knew her better than she knew herself?

Either way, it didn't matter. Not if she was going to be completely honest with herself. Jared *was* absolutely right. She hadn't accepted Leland's proposal because she was in love with him, but because of the emotional security he represented. She did love him, but not in that all-consuming way she'd once loved Jared. As he'd so graciously informed her, Leland didn't make her feel too much, didn't threaten her or turn her world upside down. Leland was safe. Not exactly fodder for happily-ever-after.

She leaned her shoulder against the window frame and sighed. She'd thought she'd been after some serious grounding and perspective when she'd called Leland from her cell phone. The truth of the matter was entirely different. In reality, she'd been looking for something much more dangerous—that certain spark, a hint of lust. Anything that remotely resembled the traitorous emotions she still felt for Jared.

All she'd gotten for her trouble had been regret and a whole lot of guilt, because no matter how much she wanted to feel otherwise, Jared's words had never rang more true. She'd felt absolutely nothing remotely like what a lover should feel upon hearing Leland's voice.

Through no fault of her own, she was going to cause Leland a great deal of embarrassment. He wasn't the type to appreciate his orderly world being twisted inside out, something her recent notoriety would certainly accomplish. Until now, she'd fit perfectly in Leland's world, and he in hers. And while the idea gave her comfort, reality sang another song, one that would croon mournfully for a passion that just didn't exist between them.

Beige.

She spun the ring around again as she looked down at the sparkling gem. She supposed she really wasn't into beige, after all.

Slowly, she slipped the engagement ring from her finger. Funny, but she didn't even miss the weight.

So did that mean she really did want red-hot and sexy, as Kellie had teased her about last Friday night?

Peyton had no future with Jared. Hell, she wasn't even sure she wanted to consider the future, period, given their present circumstances. There were too many unresolved issues between them, too much hurt and not enough trust to even begin to recapture what they'd once shared.

Nothing had really changed between them, she realized, except the passage of time. His avoidance of emotion still ran strong, as witnessed by the way he'd tried to pick a fight with her over the surname on Adam's birth certificate, followed by his attack on her reasons for agreeing to marry Leland. Instead of facing the hurt, he emotionally distanced himself from the real issue and chose another venue for his anger and pain. In fact, now that she thought about it, it made perfect sense. For someone who preferred to keep his feelings safeguarded, projecting his emotions into a safer arena allowed him to vent his frustrations without being forced to address the true issue.

And he'd had the nerve to chide her for wanting to feel safe.

Security was a subject very familiar to her. Not only physically, but emotionally, as well. After the death of her mother, Peyton's life had consisted of one foster home after the other. She'd had no other living relatives any social worker could find, so she'd been left in the care of the department of children's services. Not all of the homes she'd lived in were bad experiences. Some were even fairly decent, with good, hardworking people offering their care, if not their hearts, to the children entrusted to them. Unfortunately, through no fault of her own, she'd been bounced from

one home to the next, never allowing her
even the illusion of belonging.

On the other hand, not all of the foster
the safe havens they were supposed t(
There'd been the alcoholic foster mother whose cocktail hour started right after she set the milk and cereal
on the table at breakfast. The children in her care
walked on eggshells, never knowing when the woman
would explode into a rage, or who would be her target
of verbal abuse for the day. When the abuse went from
verbal to physical, a social worker had thankfully noticed bruises on Peyton and the other children. They'd
promptly been removed from the home.

From there, she'd gone to a new family, where her
foster parents had a teenage son who took great pleasure in torturing her and some of the other younger
children. To this day she could barely stand the sight
of a spider, and earthworms had her running for the
hills. An endless series of nightmares that had her
waking up screaming in the night had the family calling her social worker to find her yet another place to
live.

Peyton's next move had her foolishly believing
she'd finally found that safe haven she'd craved. On
the surface, everything had appeared absolutely wonderful. The house had been beautiful, the nicest she'd
ever lived in, and her foster parents had been loving
and kind, doing their best to make her feel welcome
in their home. Treating her, she'd believed, like they
would have treated their own daughter. Unfortunately,
she'd learned a valuable lesson—that nothing was
ever as it seemed. Because behind that loving pre-
tence, behind all the fine furnishings and her very first

..vate bedroom, decorated in pink-and-white, lurked an evil she hadn't seen coming.

She'd heard horrible stories from other children in the foster care system, and had taken heed of their warnings of creaking doors and floorboards in the middle of the night, signaling a nocturnal visit no child should ever have to receive. Until the Williamson home, she'd been spared that particular ugliness.

As an adult, she understood she'd been powerless, but as a child, she'd blamed herself. After several months, she'd suffered from what she now knew had been severe depression. Thankfully, her social worker eventually noticed the drastic changes in her appearance, her demeanor, as well as her grades, and instantly knew something had gone terribly wrong. For reasons Peyton still failed to understand, she'd managed to maintain enough trust to tell her social worker what was going on in the Williamson household. A degrading medical exam had given the Department of Children and Families all the proof they needed, and she was promptly removed from the home. Dr. and Mrs. Williamson were prosecuted for child molestation and a whole host of other charges she hadn't understood at the time.

It was then she'd been sent to the Biddeford Home for Girls, a move that, to this day, she firmly believed had saved her life. Without the firm but gentle guidance of the nuns who ran the home, she shuddered to think where she might have finally landed. Still, trust wasn't something that came easily for her, but thanks to the love and patience of Sister Margaret and Harry Shanks, her future hadn't been completely crippled by her past.

Looking back, Peyton figured for the most part her life could've been a whole lot worse. Security, control and most of all, trust, were important to her. Leland would have provided those for her, but she understood now that without love, their marriage would have been as empty as any stereotypical Hollywood or Capitol Hill union. She'd spent too many years with emptiness to accept anything less than real love. Something she should have realized before accepting Leland's proposal of marriage.

She closed her hand around the engagement ring. Jared couldn't offer her what she needed, either. Even if they weren't running for their lives, security and control were difficult to possess with a man who risked his life for the job. She knew and understood that about him, but she had at one time accepted it for one simple reason—she'd loved him deeply. But she had trusted him, too. While he might be a little more emotionally bankrupt than she'd have liked, he had never lied to her, had never intentionally hurt her and, most important, he had treated her feelings for him as if they were rare, treasured gifts. With Jared, she'd always known where she stood.

And how had she repaid him? By turning him over to the very men she realized now were trying to kill him. She had handed him in without waiting to hear his side of the story. What she'd told him about being forced to testify against him had been true, but the real heart of the matter was far worse. She'd done what she had to because of a selfish need that wouldn't allow her to relinquish what security and control she'd managed to gain over her life.

She didn't know if she could ever really rectify

...one to him. Words were indeed cheap, ...eserve to know the truth. Plus she owed ...logy. Neither would change the past, but ...rds came from the heart, maybe he could find it ... in his own to forgive her for not trusting him and for allowing her insecurities to rule her actions.

With the ring still clutched in her hand, she left the bedroom. She found Jared standing in front of the fireplace, his hands thrust into the front pockets of his jeans as he looked down into the flames. Other than the light from the fire, only the bluish glow of the moonlight seeping through the windows illuminated the room.

He turned his head to look at her as she walked toward him. Even in the dimly lit room, there was no mistaking the flash of lust in his sexier-than-sin eyes. Her heart pounded against her ribs.

"Looks like I'm not the only one who can't sleep tonight," he said quietly.

"We need to talk," she told him, determined to remain focused on her purpose for leaving the sanctity of the bedroom. The brief glimpse of need in his eyes was not going to deter her from her goal. She hoped. "There's something you need to know."

She came up beside him and made the mistake of looking more deeply into his eyes. Oh, yeah, that was definitely desire she saw simmering there. Regardless of her determination to remain focused, her body reacted in total and complete conflict of her goals. The enticing rasp of her hardening nipples against the soft cotton of her top made her realize just how dangerous Jared was to her sanity. She really shouldn't be surprised. If there was one area where they never had any problems, it'd been in the bedroom, or anywhere else they'd made love.

He lifted his hand and gently pushed a stray wisp of hair behind her ear, then curved his fingers around the back of her neck. "Sounds ominous."

She struggled to ignore the delicious chill that sped down her spine. "Seems like everything we do or say these days is."

She reached for his hand, the one gently massaging the base of her skull and creating one hell of a distraction. She blamed her easily sidetracked thoughts on her body's earlier sensual awakening. It had nothing whatsoever to do with her continued craving of his touch.

Turning his hand upward, she carefully laid the diamond engagement ring in his palm. One by one, she pressed his fingers around the cool gem. "You were right. I can't marry Leland. Not when I still have feelings for you. Unresolved feelings," she clarified, lest he think she was still head over heels in love with him. Which she wasn't. Well, she didn't think she was.

He glanced down at the ring before shifting his gaze back to hers. The desire shining in his eyes deepened. "What are you saying, Peyton?"

She cleared her suddenly clogged throat. "I'm saying I accepted that ring under false pretenses. The reasons aren't all that different than when I turned you over to the feds three years ago without giving you a chance to plead your case."

He shook his head and frowned. "But I thought—"

She placed her fingers over his lips to silence him.

''What I said about being forced to testify against you is true, Jared. Without the protection of marriage, I would have had no choice but to reveal anything you might have told me. But I sacrificed you, just as I was going to sacrifice myself by marrying Leland, because I refused give up what little control I did have over my life. I couldn't take a chance and trust you. If I did, and I was wrong, I would have lost everything that gave me the security I needed in my life. I couldn't let go of that. Hence the reason I owe you an apology. I betrayed your trust, Jared. It was extremely selfish, and for that I am deeply sorry.''

He glanced back at the fire. With an almost desperate need, she wanted him to accept her apology. Fearing rejection, she distanced herself by moving to the sofa and sitting down. For each second that ticked by in silence, her anxiety mounted.

What was she hoping for? Certainly nothing as ridiculous as a declaration of love. Understanding? Yes, that's what she wanted from him. Whether or not he accepted her apology, she at least needed him to understand her reasons for not giving him her complete and total faith. If he gave her that much, then perhaps someday he could actually forgive her for betraying him when he had never done anything but believe in her.

Finally, he turned to face her. Features that had been virtually etched in granite since he'd stormed back into her life were softened now, as was the look in his startling gaze. ''Do you really think you're telling me something I haven't already figured out for myself?''

She let out a breath she hadn't realized she'd been

holding. "Probably not," she admitted. *Obtuse* was not a word she could ever have used to describe Jared Romine.

"We are who we are because of what we've lived through, fought for or suffered from. I know what the Williamsons did to you, sweetheart. And I know what *that* horrific experience did to you, too, remember? You were betrayed by people you trusted to take care of you and keep you safe, so your fragile sense of security had been threatened. When you saw that threat again, you did the only thing you could do. You protected yourself the only way you knew how."

This was the Jared she'd fallen in love with, the one who'd understood her, and, once upon a time, had accepted her for who she was, idiosyncrasies, faults and all.

He gestured with his hand, still clasping the ring she'd placed there. "I also know what giving up this ring and all it entails means to you, too."

"All it means is that I can't marry a man I'm not completely in love with, no matter how much safety he can offer me. I sold out once in my life, Jared, and it cost me dearly. I'm not talking about security, but something so much more important and profound. I'm not going to repeat the same mistake twice."

"Meaning?"

"Meaning I should have trusted you then and didn't. I'm trusting you now. With my life."

He slowly walked toward her and crouched in front of her. After setting the ring on the table, he rested his hand on her thigh. A flurry of sensations shot through her body, making her breasts tingle.

"What about your heart?" he asked. "What about those unresolved feelings you mentioned?"

Said organ stopped beating, and finally resumed at a maddening pace. "My heart?" She carefully removed his hand from her thigh. "No. There's too much…everything. We're not the same people we were three years ago. Too much has happened for us to ever recapture what we once had. You found Beth. Whether or not you really were in love with her doesn't matter. You cared about her enough to marry her and try to make a life together. She meant something to you—you can't deny that."

He shifted his gaze to somewhere over her shoulder and shook his head. Whether in denial or agreement, she couldn't say.

"I lost our son," she murmured. "That's something I've had to live with. And while I doubt I'll ever suffer anything as painful in my life as losing a child, I've had to move on or run the risk of becoming one of those women who clings to the past and spends all her waking hours thinking of what might have been instead of getting on with the business of living."

"So what are you saying? That no matter what, there can never be an 'us' again?"

"You're like a drug, Jared. Being near you is like laying a needle in front of a hype in need of a fix. That's not how I want to live my life, and I refuse for us to be one of those pitiful couples you hear about that keep repeating the same mistakes over and over again because they can't let go of the past."

Or the great sex. The wayward thought came out of nowhere, but she couldn't deny the truth of it, either. Sex with Jared had always been fabulous, which made kicking the habit that much more difficult.

"No one says we have to keep making the same mistakes. What's wrong with starting fresh?"

Everything, she thought. But, oh, the temptation was tough to resist. Did they have a twelve-step program for sex?

Hello, my name is Peyton. I'm addicted to sex with a guy who is totally wrong for me.

She needed distance or else her resolve would crumble and she'd be wrapping her body around his and begging him to make that fresh start with her. Instead, she pushed him away and stood. She hadn't taken two steps when his fingers grabbed her wrist and halted her.

"Answer me, Peyton."

She looked up at him. Desire, need and something much more frightening lit his gaze. Hope.

"It's not possible," she told him. "Not after everything we've been through. Especially when we both have a bad habit of repeating history. The past would always be there, between us, against us. Whether we acknowledged it or not, it'd always guide us subconsciously, giving us no choice but to act accordingly."

"So you're just going to walk away from us?"

You did. She might have kept the words to herself, but they were a solid reminder of why she and Jared could never resume their relationship. "We have no other choice."

She attempted to shrug out of his gentle grasp, but he suddenly tightened his hold.

"Yes, we do," he said, his expression hardening. "We can choose to be together."

"Two days ago you could hardly look at me without being pissed off. Why the sudden turnabout, Jared? Nothing has changed between us."

"This isn't about change, sweetheart. It's about control, and how you're afraid to give up your hold on it."

She laughed, but the sound held no humor. "You're insane."

He let out a sigh and tugged her close. "It's not repeating the past that frightens you. It's losing what control you've managed to obtain in recent months that has you running scared. The future is uncertain, and that doesn't quite fit into your reality. If they get to us first, we might not even have a future to worry about, so what the hell is wrong with just living in the moment?"

She shook her head. Not because she didn't agree with him, but because what he was asking was too risky. If she and Jared managed a way out of the nightmare they were in, then what? Could she really afford yet another scar on her heart?

"Peyton, if I've learned anything during the past three years, it's that twenty minutes of wonderful beats the hell out of a lifetime of nothing."

He had a point she couldn't deny, especially since there was a damn good chance she and Jared could be killed. They might have managed so far to outrun those after them, but there were no guarantees about how much longer their luck would continue to hold. Based on what she now knew, there were a lot of reasons for them to want Jared silenced, and by extension, her as well.

Jamie Denton

In other words, what did she have to lose, much, as far as she could determine.

Keeping that thought firmly planted in her mind, she inched closer and slipped her free hand around his neck. She'd deal with tomorrow, and any regrets she might have, if and when they came. For now, twenty minutes of wonderful sounded like a good start to a splendid idea.

"Kiss me, Jared. Before I change my mind."

A welcoming smile instantly curved his mouth. "I thought you'd never ask."

12

JARED SLID PEYTON'S OTHER hand around his neck. She laced her fingers together, bringing her body closer to his. Her nipples hardened beneath her top, teasing him. Her warm scent enticed him. The feel of her body against his made his erection pulse and throb in delicious anticipation.

Peyton was finally in his arms where she belonged. A Peyton without restrictions, without the symbol of her pledge to another man between them—or anything else, for that matter, except perhaps a past they could not change and a future of uncertainty. Toss in the gut-wrenching emotions he knew deep in his soul would never fade, and it spelled only one thing: spending the rest of his life making up for the past.

She was his life. She was his love. She was his soul mate. Then, now and always. All he had to do was convince her of what had remained in his heart all the months they'd been separated. Yes, he had married another woman, and while he'd cared deeply for Beth, she hadn't been Peyton. He wasn't a complete jackass. Beth did hold a special place in his heart, but that space remained crowded by guilt that she had died protecting him when he hadn't deserved her loyalty. Worse, she'd died knowing he could never completely love her because his heart would always remain with another woman. With Peyton.

Now was not the time for regrets. Not when he had the woman he'd always loved rubbing her body against his in an ancient siren's call. He had two immediate needs—kissing her senseless and freeing them of their clothing posthaste. If he didn't feel the press of her satiny soft skin against him soon, he'd go crazy.

He smoothed his hands down her backside to cup her bottom. She sighed and wiggled against his hands. "Kiss me, Jared."

No way was he letting her go now that he'd finally gotten her back where she belonged. He dipped his head and caught her lips with his. She opened immediately, inviting him inside the sweet warmth of her mouth, where her tongue danced and mated with his. She suckled his tongue. Her hands slid into his hair, holding him so he couldn't withdraw. She arched her slender body against his. His erection throbbed painfully behind the fly of his jeans.

He removed one hand from her bottom to reach beneath her top and palm her breast. He swallowed her soft moan of pleasure as he rasped his thumb over the pebble hardness of her nipple. The need to taste her, to draw her into his mouth and suckle overwhelmed him. A need he could barely contain when she suddenly broke the kiss and pulled away from him.

He nearly panicked, thinking she'd changed her mind after all...until he focused on her face and saw a slow, seductive smile curving her lips, and a blazing need flare in her periwinkle eyes, turning them a deeper shade of blue. Those luscious eyes said it all. There would be no turning back tonight.

She reached for the bottom edge of her crop top and slowly began to lift the fabric, exposing rich creamy skin, inch by delectable inch. The smile on her face was nothing short of wicked as she tossed the top somewhere over her shoulder. Next, she toyed with the plaid bottoms, running her middle finger between the fabric and her tummy. His mouth went dry when her whole hand dipped beneath the edge of elastic.

"Umm," she murmured. "You should feel how wet your kiss has made me."

The rate of his heartbeat increased to dangerous levels. He tried to speak, but the words lodged in his throat. All he could emit was a low moan of combined pleasure and frustration.

"Do you remember how you could make me come just by touching me...here?"

Did he ever. His fingers flexed in response.

"Do you want to touch me, Jared?"

Her throaty whisper nearly had him coming. He cleared his throat. "Yes," he managed to rasp.

"Then take off your clothes," she ordered.

She could've asked him to swing from the rafters and he'd have done it if it meant being able to touch her again. He did as she requested, understanding her need to be in control. For now, he thought. Later, he'd show her what it meant to really lose that control she guarded so carefully.

Within seconds he shed his clothes, then stood waiting for her next command. The appreciation in her eyes warmed him a thousand times more than the heat from the flames crackling in the hearth. No matter what tomorrow brought, tonight they would have this moment, where only the two of them existed in a heated convergence of heart, body and soul.

She tugged on the loose-fitting pajama bottoms, and they landed in a puddle of blue-and-pink plaid cotton at her feet. "I've changed my mind," she said, moving toward him. "I don't want you to touch me... yet."

She stepped past him and snagged a pillow from the sofa before coming back around to stand in front of him. The pillow hit the floor at his feet. His erection bobbed in anticipation as she settled to her knees in front of him.

She slipped both hands around his penis and began a rhythmic massage. "I'm going to taste you. Can you handle it?"

"I'll handle anything you want to give," he rasped. "I'm yours to do with as you please."

"Umm," she said, bringing her mouth closer to the swollen tip. Her warm breath fanned him. "Anything?"

He sucked in a sharp breath as she used the tip of her tongue to circle the head. "Anything," he croaked despite the dryness of his throat.

She chuckled before taking him in her mouth, making cardiac arrest a distinct possibility as she slid her lips farther down his shaft.

Her hands clutched his backside, kneading his flesh while urging him to move his hips in a gentle thrusting motion. With each thrust, she took him deeper, using her tongue and her lips to drive him wild.

Her throat closed around him, drawing him deeper,

milking the moisture from his body. His legs trembled. With nothing to hold on to for support, he dug his fingers into her honey-blond hair. He heard a moan, but he was too lost in the sensations rippling through his body to know which of them made that low, mournful sound.

The pressure built, and he knew that if he didn't stop her, he would come in an explosion of heat. Yet he couldn't bear to put an end to her sweet brand of lovemaking, so he let her have her way with him. Her hands moved from his backside to cup his sac. Using her nails, she gently scraped her fingers along the underside of his testicles, heightening his pleasure to the point where he could take it no longer.

He tried to push her mouth away, but she was insistent, pressing him harder toward completion. Unable to bear the exquisite torture another second, he shuddered as he tried to hold back, but she refused to relinquish her control over him. He came in a rush. The world stopped spinning as she took all he had to give.

Tremors continued to wrack his body as she slowly brought him back to that place where he could hear the sounds of their ragged breathing and feel his own heart beating a rapid cadence in his chest.

Slowly, she kissed her way up his body until she was standing on the pillow, nibbling his jaw as he tried to regulate his breathing. Her hands slid into his hair and he banded his arms around her, pulling her close. There were a thousand things he wanted to say to her, but he sensed her need for another type of communication, so he remained silent.

Despite the weakness in his legs, he bent and

scooped her up in his arms. He considered taking her to the bedroom, but that could wait until later. Right now he wanted her as mindless as she'd made him. Besides, lengthy foreplay would give his weakened body a chance to renew itself.

Peyton wasn't exactly sure where she'd expected Jared to take her, but the overstuffed chair in front of the fire had not entered her mind's list of places for making love. Of course, with Jared, anything was possible. She very fondly recalled an incident with unlit tapers that had been highly erotic and incredibly satisfying.

She looked into his eyes as he gently set her down. He quickly positioned the chair so she faced the fire, then sank to his knees in front of her.

"Do you trust me?" he asked as he used both hands to scoot her bottom toward the center of the cushion.

Instinct told her his question went beyond sex, but she didn't want to go there. Not now, when her emotions were running rampant and her body hummed with anticipation. Later, much later, would be a more appropriate time for that kind of reflection and consideration. All she wanted was Jared inside her, loving her. Still, she had a moment's hesitation before she slowly nodded.

A lazy grin canted his mouth. "Good answer, sweetheart." His hands slid from her bottom to her thighs, his fingers tenderly kneading her flesh.

Then one hand moved from her thigh to the curve behind her knee. Carefully, he lifted her leg and placed it over the arm of the chair.

She tensed. "Jared?"

"Trust me, sweetheart." He placed a kiss on her

inner thigh. "I'm going to take you someplace you haven't been to in a very long time." He repeated the process with her other leg until she was lying in the chair, completely exposed to him.

She closed her eyes and leaned her head back while Jared's fingers gently massaged her flesh. Each time the back of his hand brushed against her moist core, her hips jerked toward him.

He chuckled. "Not just yet, sweetheart. We haven't even begun this journey."

The sound of his voice soothed her, as well as filled her with an excitement born of sensual promise.

She heard the rasp of leather and opened her eyes. He was standing with the leather belt from his jeans in his hand. "What do you think you're going to do with that?" She couldn't help feel slightly alarmed. She was turned on, most definitely, but the teasing glint in his eyes made her wary.

"Not what you're thinking," he said with a soft chuckle. "Relax, Peyton. I haven't picked up any strange or dominating sexual habits recently."

Not exactly reassured, she kept a close eye on the leather belt in his hands.

"Lie back again and close your eyes," he ordered gently.

He knelt before her, so she did as he instructed. Then nearly leaped out of the chair when she felt the glide of smooth, soft leather against her center, followed by the silken slide of his tongue over her clitoris. The combination of sensations as he rhythmically repeated the process had her panting. She couldn't remember the last time she'd ever felt anything so incredibly stimulating. His thumb rested at her opening, teasing her as he gently slipped it inside—only enough to make her body yearn for more.

She arched her back and tried to press her hips forward, her body needing, demanding more of the exquisite pleasure.

His lips kissed the flat of her belly as the strange softness of the tip of his leather belt slid against her. "You are so wet," he murmured against her flesh. "Wet and ready to come for me, aren't you, baby?"

"Jared," she cried, begging him to give her the release her body so desperately sought.

"Not just yet. Now open your eyes."

She did, and was at first stunned by the fierce light of possession shining in his green gaze. An odd sense of comfort quickly followed.

"I want you to watch," he said. "See how your body responds to my touch?"

Her arms trembled in protest as she pushed herself upward so she could fulfill Jared's intimate request. She hardly believed it possible, but the sharp tug of need in her belly pulled harder, demanding and insistent. How was it that the sight of his long slim fingers slipping in and out of her moist heat made her even more aroused?

"You like watching me, don't you?"

The only sound she could make that even resembled coherency was a sharp moan of intense pleasure. She watched in fascination as he discarded the belt, then added another finger to the two already inside her, pushing deep and making her cry out as every single nerve ending in her body came alive with sensation.

She pulsed around his fingers. His eyes darkened as he dipped his head and placed an openmouthed kiss over her, his velvety soft tongue whirling around her swollen clitoris, driving her closer to where pure satisfaction awaited.

He eased back ever so slightly until he could look into her eyes. The intensity of his gaze held her spellbound, while her heart rate soared into the danger zone. Her body trembled with the need for release. The sight of his tongue laving her, the feel of his fingers drawing her moisture were too much. Just when she thought she couldn't hold back another second, he stopped suddenly, and was looming over her before her mind could assimilate the changes.

Stretched above her with hands gripping the arms of the chair, he eased himself inside her. Exposed as she was, she felt every glorious inch of him as he entered her deeply. She cried out as he thrust over and over again, pushing her into mindless wonder. The intensity of her orgasm gripped her hard, shook her body to its very core. He continued to rock against her, driving into her relentlessly as her body poised for yet another release.

They came together like a crashing wave. Her fierce cries of pleasure were barely perceptible over his deep groans at his own powerful release.

Somehow, in the sensual fog, they made it to the rug in front of the hearth, their bodies entangled as they soothed and gently explored each other at their leisure.

As much as she hated to admit it even to herself, she had desperately missed this part of her life with Jared—the closeness and intimacy. No matter what demons from the past haunted them, when they came together in love, nothing could hurt them. Their months apart faded away as she snuggled closer in his embrace.

Their future might be uncertain, but Peyton knew without a doubt that somehow her future would include Jared.

JUST AFTER TEN the next morning, Peyton woke to the heavenly aromas of frying bacon, baking bread and fresh-brewed coffee. The scents wafted into the bedroom, drawing her reluctantly out of her slumber. She smiled. The bedroom wasn't the only place she considered Jared a whiz. He made the best eggs Benedict east of the Mississippi.

She threw back the covers and crawled out of the warmth of the bed to fumble with her bag for clothes and other essentials. A hot shower was definitely in order before she faced Jared. With any luck, she'd ease some of the ache from all those dormant muscles that had been reawakened with a vengeance, thanks to him. The memory of how she'd gotten into such a state made her smile widen.

The night spent in Jared's arms had been nothing short of glorious, she admitted as she stepped beneath the stinging spray from the showerhead. As a lover, he'd never left her wanting—unless, of course, it was for more of his scrumptious brand of lovemaking. Of that, she could never seem to get enough.

Last night there had been something more to their coming together. Something infinitely emotional and definitely more intense. She suspected part of the intensity may have had to do with the fact that they were running for their lives, but she sensed the closeness they'd shared went beyond their skewed reality. Not only had he said he loved her, but he had shown her over and over again, each time twice as sweet and tender as the last.

She dipped her head beneath the spray. Once they were able to reclaim their lives, she still hadn't a clue what would happen to them, or rather, their future. She had her own demons to wrestle with, and one of those included a discussion with Leland. After what the press was doing to her reputation by linking her to Jared and his alleged crimes, Leland might even refuse to see her. Considering how he absolutely despised having his neat and orderly environment ruffled, it was a possibility she had to consider, and maybe even accept.

Assuming she and Jared did manage to clear their names, she didn't have a moment of doubt that her job with the Justice Department would be history. *But what about Jared?* she thought, lathering her hair. He had said he had no qualms about returning to the bureau. According to him, the FBI itself wasn't bad, just those on the inside using the agency for their own personal agenda. The one thing she was having difficulty reconciling wasn't so much that he would return to the bureau if he could, but that he might once again carry a badge, disappear for weeks on end without a single word, and keep that part of his life separate from his life with her. In other words, she wasn't sure she wanted to return to the status quo. If they were going to resume their relationship, she needed things to be different this time. If not, they would end up being one of those pitiful couples people talked about.

She gave herself a mental shake as she rinsed her hair and left the shower. There would be time later for thoughts of the future. Right now they needed to come up with a plan on how to expose those involved in the conspiracy. Their personal life would just have to wait.

Ten minutes later she emerged from the bedroom. Upon entering the living room, the first thing she noted was that all evidence of their lovemaking had been effectively erased. No stray articles of clothing, no furniture out of place. Even the pillows they'd scattered in front of the hearth, where they'd made love again at a much more leisurely and exploratory pace, had been returned to their proper spot. If it hadn't been for the aching tenderness between her legs, she might have believed she'd dreamed the entire, delicious night of passion in the arms of the man she loved.

She headed into the kitchen to see if Jared needed some help with breakfast, and came to a dead stop when she reached the doorway. Instead of finding Jared, as she'd expected, Harry was opening the oven door and retrieving fresh-baked rolls. Disappointment rolled through her as her heart sank clear to the toes of her cheap sneakers.

"Where's Jared?" she asked, but she already knew. She knew, and it hurt her right to the core of her soul.

Harry closed the oven door and set the rolls on the counter next to the stove before turning to face her. His sympathetic gaze only confirmed the news. Jared had left.

"He didn't want you to be alone," Harry told her.

She crossed her arms. "That explains why you came back," she said. "Where is Jared?" She despised the telltale sharpness of her tone, but disappointment did that to a woman.

Harry let out a sigh and gestured to the small round table in the dining area. "You better sit down, Peyton."

She narrowed her gaze. "Dammit, Harry. What's going on?"

"He went back to D.C. this morning."

"Back to... But why?"

He poured them each a cup of coffee, then carried the mugs to the table, waiting patiently for her to join him. "He knew you'd be upset," he said.

"Upset?" She remained in the doorway, not trusting her legs to carry her. Of all the stupid, asinine places for Jared to go, marching right into the lion's den had to top the list. "Upset doesn't even begin to catalog what I'm feeling right now. Furious is closer to the truth." And disappointed beyond belief.

Instead of looking at her, Harry concentrated on stirring creamer into his coffee. "He's only doing what he thinks is best for you."

"Oh, screw that," she retorted. She marched across the kitchen and dropped into the chair opposite Harry. "Jared is doing what Jared always does. Whatever is the easiest and least complicated for him, and to hell with what anyone else thinks."

While she seethed, Harry took a few sips of coffee, before wandering back to the stove. He heaped two plates with fluffy scrambled eggs and crisp bacon, just the way she liked them. "You're not being fair to him."

She looked up as Harry set the food in front of her. "He's going to get himself killed," she said more calmly. "These people, they're ruthless."

He settled his hand on her shoulder and gave it a

gentle squeeze. "Trust him. He knows what he's doing."

Trust him? She'd thought she could. Unfortunately, she'd just been taught otherwise.

She waited until Harry was seated across from her. "What did he say to you?" she demanded.

"Not much."

That sure as hell didn't surprise her.

"Just that he was going back to D.C. now that he had enough evidence to hopefully put an end to this mess."

She shook her head. "That's insane. All the so-called evidence is at best circumstantial. What does he think he's going to do? He can't go to the bureau. There's no one there he can trust, if his suspicions are right and someone high up in the chain of command is involved. God, Harry. He's going to get himself killed for sure this time."

Her friend gave her a level stare. "Peyton, listen to me. You need to have a little faith in him. He knows what he's doing."

Her fork clattered against the plate as it slipped from her fingers. "If he knew what he was doing, he would've been able to put an end to this mess a long time ago."

"You're worrying about something where you have no control. Besides, you can pace the carpet bare and you know it's not going to change anything."

"Worrying about Jared has been as natural as drawing my next breath for too many years. I've done nothing but be frightened for his safety since the day he became a part of my life."

Was Harry right? Was she having a self-righteous

snit because she had no control in a situation so completely insane she didn't know what to do next? Or was it something much more basic? Like Jared's leaving without talking to her first? Without reassuring her as best he could that he would take every precaution to ensure their future together? She suspected both, but in her current state of mind, she leaned more heavily toward the latter.

"Why couldn't he have told me himself?" she mused aloud. "After..." After all that talk of trust the past few days, he should have at least been up front with her and let her know what he had planned.

Damn him!

Harry lifted his mug and took a sip of the steamy coffee. "I'm sure he thought he was doing what was best."

Regardless of Harry's attempt to placate her, Peyton realized that once again Jared had acted true to form. He'd left her feeling helpless, alone, and worst of all, with nothing to hang on to other than a few sweet whispered words of love spoken during the dark of night.

13

By ONE O'CLOCK Monday afternoon, Sunny was heading north on the coast highway from Charleston, on her way to Cole Harbor, South Carolina. Her orders: to interview the last agent to work the Romine case, Chase Bracken.

The assignment had come as a complete surprise, especially since she'd already been requested by the assistant director to be a part of the team investigating Theodore Galloway for the Senate Judicial Committee's hearings that would take place later next month. Just this morning, on her drive to the airport in D.C., she'd heard the president's announcement regarding the appointment of Galloway to the Supreme Court. Instead of traveling, she should have spent the day in meetings with dozens of other agents, going over the various assignments for the background investigation of Galloway.

She exited the highway and took the turnoff for Cole Harbor. If she'd learned anything the last few days, it was to expect the unexpected. For any agent with designs on upward mobility within the bureau, being chosen by her superiors for such a sensitive investigation was quite the coup. It meant she'd been noticed...in a good way. The fact that she'd been asked again to work on the Romine case was a dream job as far as her puzzle-solving mind was concerned.

She reached the town limits of Cole Harbor and simply followed all the Go, Fight, Win, Cougars signs to the local high school, where Bracken now worked as a football coach and teacher. She had plenty of questions for the former agent, but the most curious item on her list was what would make a seasoned agent with a reputation like Bracken's walk away from his career. She didn't need her degree in criminal justice to know it had something to do with his association with Romine's sister. Sunny had a few other suspicions and hoped to have them confirmed, as well.

She parked in a vacant spot near the administration building. Inside, the halls were cool and relatively deserted. The slam of a locker door, followed by the sound of sneakers hitting the asphalt tiles, came from somewhere down another corridor. She located the main office and within minutes was directed to a classroom on the third floor.

The door was open, so she stepped inside the darkened room. Her eyes quickly adjusted to the dimness in the place, lit only by the glare of the movie screen set up at the front of the classroom. Agent Bracken stood at the back of the room behind a slide projector. On the screen were the faces of infamous serial killers known as the Hillside Stranglers, who'd ravaged much of the Southern California area during the late seventies.

Obviously she'd walked into Bracken's course on criminal justice. There was no other logical explanation she could come up with for why he'd be telling his class about such two notorious killers.

Bracken shut down the projector. "Lights, please," he said, just as the bell sounded, announcing the end of the period. Surprisingly, none of the students rushed to their feet. From the bureau photos Sunny had inspected just that morning, there was no mistaking that Bracken qualified as a hunk. No doubt half the girls in his class were in love with him, while the guys all wanted to be like him. Not that she could blame them. Bracken had one hell of a reputation, and the charisma to pull it off, when he chose to use it.

The overhead fluorescent fixtures buzzed and came to life. Sunny found herself staring into the intense lilac eyes of former Special Agent Chase Bracken. The photos didn't even begin to do the man justice. Well over six feet tall, he was built like a linebacker, with movie-star good looks. Simply put, the man was stunningly gorgeous, if a gal was interested in the big and bulky type boasting a lady-killer grin.

"That's it for today," he said to the class, but he was looking in her direction with a very unwelcome frown drawing his midnight-black eyebrows together.

"Interesting topic," she said once the students filed out of the room. "A little gruesome for teens, don't you think?"

Bracken shrugged and started rolling up the cord for the slide projector's remote control. "The kids eat the stuff up. It's all part of the death penalty discussions that'll take place later this week." He laid the cord over the machine and gave her a hard look that matched his granite features. "Not that what I do is the bureau's business any longer."

Sunny grinned nervously. "That obvious, huh?"

"That obvious. So what can I do for you, Agent...?"

She didn't let the fact that Bracken failed to return her smile stop her from closing the space between them and extending her hand in greeting. "MacGregor," she said. "Sunny MacGregor."

At least he shook her hand, she thought. "I'd like to ask you a few questions about your investigation of Jared Romine."

He let out a sigh filled with impatience. "My final report is in the file." He turned his back to her and began gathering papers and placing them in a brand-new leather briefcase that still squeaked when opened.

"Yes," she said. "About that report. I've read it. What I'm interested in is what's not in the report, Agent Bracken."

He braced his hands on the desk and turned his head, giving her a steely glare. "*Former* Agent Bracken," he said in a rough tone. "I left the bureau, remember?"

"Yes, well..." She cleared her throat, not the least bit intimidated by him. Not much, anyway. "Now why is that, do you think? You were a decorated agent. I agree with the reports that some of your methods left a little to be desired on occasion, but I don't think there's anyone who can deny you produced positive results. The bureau likes results, so what would make a man walk away from a fast-track career? From all appearances, you were headed straight for the top, yet you threw it all way."

He turned and rested his backside against the metal desk, crossing his arms over his wide chest. "Retirement sounded like a good idea."

"I don't buy that, Agent Bracken."

"It's *Mr.* Bracken or *Coach* Bracken," he said coldly. "I'm no longer an agent."

"Okay, *Coach* Bracken. Why walk away like you did?"

"Look, as I told the last jackass that was here, I quit. No big deal. I decided I was ready for a change. End of story. Now if you'll excuse me, I have a gym class in forty minutes."

There had been other agents sent to question him? Why hadn't she been informed? If she'd known in advance she wasn't the first sent to speak to him, she would have altered her approach. "What other jackass?"

"The other agent here this morning," he said impatiently.

"There was an another agent here? To question you about your investigation of the Romine files?"

"Sunny, huh? Guess they call you that because you're so bright."

She didn't appreciate his sarcasm. Not when she was on the verge of discovering something vitally important. Anticipation buzzed inside her. "Please stick to the questions, Coach Bracken. Do you know the name of this other agent?"

He reached behind him and pulled a business card from the side pocket of his briefcase. "Caffey. Marcus Caffey," he said, handing her the card. "He's out of the New York field office."

"This is highly unusual," she murmured while inspecting the card. She looked back at Chase. "May I ask what you told Agent Caffey?"

"Same thing I'm telling you. I quit. End of story."

She had to find a way to get through to him so he'd tell her what he knew. Every instinct told her Bracken had walked away from his career in the bureau because he'd learned information that could prove Romine's innocence. But if that was the case, then why didn't he bring that information to light and put an end to the manhunt for Romine, and now Douglas?

"Coach Bracken, I have reason to believe that Jared Romine is innocent. I also believe that you agree with me, which is a part of what facilitated your retirement from the bureau."

The look in his eyes turned glacial. She had him, and they both knew it. "You assume a lot."

"Agents like you don't walk away from the job just because retirement sounds good. They walk away when they no longer trust or believe in the system they've sworn to uphold. And agents like Romine don't kill their partners or top senatorial aides."

Bracken stood and picked up his briefcase. "Like I said, you assume a lot, MacGregor. Here's some advice. Go back to whoever sent you and tell them you couldn't find anything. It might just keep you alive."

He started for the door. She followed on his heels. "Then you *do* know something."

He kept walking. "I didn't say that."

"Not in so many words."

"Not in *any* words, MacGregor."

She practically had to jog to keep up with his long-legged stride. "Why won't you talk to me? I'm on your side. I'm here to help Agent Romine."

He stopped at the edge of the stairwell and looked down at her. "Are you? Who gave you this assignment? How do you know they're not using you as a pawn to gather information to use against him?''

"Did you tell Agent Caffey the same thing you're telling me?''

"No.''

She looked up at him and waited.

"Because I know who sent Caffey,'' he replied.

A slight lift of her eyebrows was the only response she gave him.

"Elijah Pelham,'' he said, then started down the stairs.

Sunny's mind started spinning as she tried to keep up with Bracken. She'd met Pelham once and hadn't liked him much. He was an officious, self-important little creep, the same rank as Gibson Russell. Both Pelham and Gib worked directly under the supervision of Vivien Kent. A coincidence? Not with an agency that liked to pride itself on its efficiency. The right hand of the bureau usually always knew what the left hand was doing.

So what was she doing here if another agent had already been sent to question Bracken? She didn't like the answer, or that Bracken could be right.

At the bottom of the first flight, she reached for Bracken's arm to slow him down. Her fingers slipped over his forearm, and thankfully, he stopped. "I need your help,'' she told him. "Agent Romine needs my help if he's going to get out of this alive, and I can't do that if you won't at least tell me what you know.''

"What makes you think I know anything, Mac-Gregor?''

"You wouldn't have quit the bureau otherwise.

You made your decision in order to save his life, didn't you?''

He let out a long sigh. "My reasons are none of your business."

"Dammit, he and Peyton Douglas will be killed if the men trying to frame him find him before I do," she said in a harsh whisper. "What are you going to tell Dr. Romine? That you had a chance to keep her brother alive for a little while longer and you refused?"

He muttered something vile, then glanced down at his wristwatch. "You have thirty minutes to convince me. And you'd better make it convincing, MacGregor. I don't suffer fools lightly."

She let out a sigh of relief and flashed him a smile. "I don't expect you do, Agent Bracken. Now if we could start by you directing me to a telephone so I can call in to let my supervisor know I wasn't able to come up with any new information, then we can begin to compare notes."

BY THE TIME THE SUN had set along the Maine coast, Peyton's anger hadn't waned one iota. How could Jared have taken off without talking to her first? She had no idea where he'd gone, whom he planned to talk to or what she was supposed to do besides sit and wait. The waiting was killing her. The anger kept her from slipping into a full-blown panic.

All morning and afternoon she'd alternated between pacing the carpet in front of the fireplace and sitting on the front porch of the cottage, listening to the waves crash upon the shore. She'd kept her cell phone turned on and with her at all times just in case Jared tried to reach her, but instinct told her he wouldn't. Whenever he'd gone on an assignment, she'd never had any contact with him. She sure as hell didn't expect him to break his code of silence now, especially when both of their lives weren't worth a nickel until this mess was over and done.

Harry had remained at the cottage with her and was inside cooking something for dinner that she probably wouldn't be able to eat, anyway. He didn't keep a television set in the cabin, so all she had as far as news came from brief sound bytes in between golden oldies from one of the local radio stations. The only news of any interest was the president's appointment of Theodore Galloway to the Supreme Court. A chill had run up her spine when she'd heard the announcement. The wheels had been set into motion. There would be no turning back now until either Jared managed to expose the bastards or they got to her and Jared and silenced them.

She tugged the faded, handmade quilt snugly over her shoulders and rested her head against the wicker chair nearest the railing of the front porch. Tucked in a cocoon of false security, with the added comfort of the loaded pistol they'd taken from the punk who'd tried to rob them resting on her lap, she laughed at the irony. Security and comfort, two emotions she'd foolishly tried to believe in when she'd spent the night in Jared's arms.

She shook her head at her foolishness. She might not regret making love to him, but she did regret letting her heart play an active role in her decision. There'd been little doubt of the fact they could never have a future together, and his running off today just cemented that belief more firmly in her mind. So if she knew all that, then why did she feel as if her heart had been ripped out of her chest?

The answer had her vision blurring with tears. She loved Jared, always had. And just her rotten luck, she probably always would. *You can't pick who you fall in love with.* That was something she recalled her mother saying often, whenever Peyton had raised the subject of her father. When her mother had died from complications arising from a serious bout of pneumonia, Peyton had overheard the doctors saying that she no longer had the will to live. Peyton had been too young to understand, but as she'd gotten older, she realized that her mother had probably died of a broken heart. She'd always said how much she loved Peyton's father, and when he'd walked away and never looked back, everything in their lives had changed.

If she took her feelings for Jared into consideration, Peyton finally understood how her mother could have given up hope. But she wasn't her mother, she thought. She would go on, just as she had when Jared had disappeared the last time.

The distinct sound of the snapping of a dried reed had her sitting up straight. Her fingers slipped around the small gun in her lap. Carefully, she removed the safety and eased the slide back to load the bullet into the chamber.

Two shadows suddenly appeared at the steps, the smaller of the two obviously female. It was the woman's large companion that worried Peyton.

"Take another step and it'll be your last," she said, leveling the weapon at the intruders. The calm note of authority in her tone surprised her, especially since her insides were quivering like Santa's mythical bowl-full-of-jelly tummy. "Who are you and what do you want?"

"Ms. Douglas, I'm Sunny MacGregor with the FBI."

Fear threatened to choke her. She was as good as dead. "Not a good answer," she managed to croak.

"Peyton, it's Chase Bracken. I'm—"

"I know who you are, Mr. Bracken." He was Dee Romine's lover, according to Jared.

"Then you know you can trust me."

"I don't know any such thing," she said truthfully. "Mind telling me what you're doing keeping company with the feds?"

"I'm here to help, Peyton."

His voice was smooth and calm, and he kept repeating her name as though she was some crazed shooter he had to talk down. He might no longer officially be with the bureau, but he obviously still had the skills.

"Where's Jared?" he asked.

She laughed, the sound caustic and brittle even to her own ears. "That's the question of the day, it seems."

"Ms. Douglas," Sunny said in the same calming tone Chase had used. "Would you mind lowering your weapon, please?"

Instead of doing as she asked, Peyton stood. If she'd learned anything the past few days, it was that nothing was as it seemed, so she planned to take no chances with her life. "I want to see ID. Now," she ordered.

"Toss it over here. Try anything stupid, and I *will* put a bullet through you."

Both Sunny and Chase did as she asked. Keeping her eyes, and the gun, on them, she stooped to retrieve the leather ID holders they'd tossed at her feet.

Although convinced of their identities, she refused to put the gun away until they answered her questions. "Okay, you are who you say you are. But that still doesn't mean I can trust you. How did you find me here? No one knows about this place."

"We did a search of public records," Sunny explained. "Your son was born at St. Andrew's Hospital in Biddeford."

"We're forty miles away from Biddeford. That still doesn't explain how you found me."

"Your medical records from the hospital told us your emergency contact was Harry Shanks. Actually, we were looking for him, hoping he'd provide us with information on where to locate you and Romine. One of the sisters at the Biddeford home told us he often comes here, and mentioned you stayed with him for a few months before your baby was born."

"Peyton, we came to help," Chase repeated.

She tapped the leather wallets containing Sunny's and Chase's identification against her thigh. She'd made the wrong choice once where Jared was concerned. To betray him yet again was not something she wanted to spend the rest of her life regretting. Still, she couldn't forget the fact that the night they'd left D.C., he'd told her if anything happened, she was to make her way to Cole Harbor and Chase Bracken. Chase would know what to do, Jared had insisted.

Slowly, she lowered the gun and engaged the

safety. "Come inside and we can talk. I hope you're hungry," she said, handing them back their IDs. "When Harry's upset or worried, he cooks. A lot. He's been frying chicken for the past two hours, so I know there's more than enough food to feed a small army."

She led the way into the cottage. Under the soft lamplight, she was able to get a good look at Sunny and Chase. Sunny was a perfect name for the petite blond agent, she thought, as she held the door for Chase to enter. He, on the other hand, was a big guy, easily four inches taller than Jared.

"Does Jared's sister know you're here?" she asked him.

A wry grin canted his mouth, and his lilac eyes softened. "Yeah," he said, "Dee knows. She wanted to be here, but one of her patients is about ready to go into labor. She did give me a message for you, though."

"She did? For me?" Peyton was surprised, as she'd never met Jared's younger sister.

Chase nodded. "She said to tell you she's anxious to meet the woman who stole her brother's heart."

Peyton offered up a wobbly smile. Someday. Maybe. Provided they got out of this alive.

14

THE WAY HE SAW IT, Jared had only one option available to him, regardless of the risk to his own life, and possibly Peyton's, as well. But he'd made a decision that consisted of finding someone to believe his story now that he had all but one of the pieces in place. Unfortunately, time had definitely run out, now that the formal announcement of Galloway's appointment to the high court had been made public.

At precisely nine o'clock, Jared parked Harry's Jeep in the first unattended public parking garage he could find deep in the heart of the city. After a cursory glance around the area to make certain he wasn't being watched, he stepped from the vehicle and reached under the seat for the pistol Harry had insisted he take with him.

With the gun tucked in the waistband of his jeans and hidden by this worn, leather bomber jacket, he gathered the envelope of evidence from the passenger seat. Keeping to the shadows as much as possible, without drawing unwanted attention, he walked the short distance to Fifteenth Street, then hurried two more blocks to the offices of the *Washington Post*. He'd never been a friend of the media; in fact, he viewed most of the reporters on the bureau beat as a colossal pain in the ass, and had always done his best to avoid talking to them. When an agent worked undercover assignments, the last thing he needed was for his face to be plastered on the front page of every newspaper in the country, with a story congratulating or condemning him for doing his job.

Despite the late hour, the main door was unlocked. If Jared's luck continued to hold, there just might be a reporter still in the building.

A security guard sat behind an enormous marble monstrosity that served as a reception desk. Jared gave a moment's thought to ignoring the guard and heading straight for the elevators, but something that reckless practically guaranteed that cops would be storming the building in no time flat.

He walked up to the heavyset guard. "I need to talk to one of your reporters."

The guard set down on a sheet of waxed paper a tuna sandwich oozing mayonnaise. "Your name?" he asked, using the back of his hand to wipe his mouth.

Jared thought about lying, but figured he'd get further with the truth. "Jared Romine."

The guard narrowed his eyes slightly, but didn't reach for the holstered revolver at his side. Jared took that as a good sign. After only a brief hesitation, the guard picked up the phone and punched in four numbers.

Jared breathed a sigh of relief. The rent-a-cop could have easily dialed the local police or even the bureau, no doubt collecting a hefty reward for the arrest and conviction of one of the FBI's biggest embarrassments. Thankfully, the guy was loyal to his employer and the "if it bleeds it leads" mentality of the news media.

"Jared Romine to see Mr. Stanton," the guard said into the receiver. "Yes, sir, he sure did." The guard paused for a moment. "No, I didn't ask for ID, but it's him." Another pause. "Right away."

"Go on up," the guard said as he hung up the phone. "Third floor. Ford Stanton will be waiting for you."

Jared thanked the guard. Within moments he stepped off the elevator onto the third floor. A tall, young, athletic looking reporter stood in the corridor waiting for him. "Jared Romine?"

Jared nodded. "Stanton?" he asked cautiously. He'd never seen the guy before, which meant he'd never had the opportunity to step on his toes. Another stroke of luck—good luck for a change.

The guy grinned from ear to ear. "I have a feeling tonight's going to be the defining moment in my career," he said as he pumped Jared's hand.

A half grin tipped Jared's mouth at the reporter's eagerness for a hot story. Heaven must be really on his side tonight. "Then you know who I am?"

Stanton sobered immediately. "There isn't a reporter in town who hasn't followed your story. Let's go somewhere we can talk."

Jared followed Stanton to a small private conference room and declined the offer for coffee. Stanton disappeared long enough to retrieve a tape recorder, an arsenal of blank tapes and a yellow legal pad, along with a half-dozen pencils.

Jared settled in the standard desk chair for what was going to be a very long conversation.

"One question before we get started," Stanton said. "Why come to the *Post?*"

"Because the *Post* has a reputation for never running scared from a political scandal," he stated honestly. He leaned forward and rested his arms on the table. "And what I'm about to tell you will sure as hell stir up a whole lot of trouble."

Stanton's grin returned with a vengeance. "Sounds like my kind of story."

ONE OF THE PERKS of working as a close personal aide to Senator Martin Phipps was going to the round of parties the senator failed to personally attend. More often than not, Phipps sent Steve in his stead to offer his apologies, usually stating an urgent business matter that required his attention at the last minute. Tonight's celebration honoring Theodore Galloway and his appointment to the U.S. Supreme Court was no exception.

Steve sipped Dom Pérignon from an elegant crystal flute, feeling more in his element than ever before. He held back a smile. If only the esteemed guests at the party knew the senator's urgent last-minute business consisted of a room at the Horton in the company of a "date" that charged a hefty hourly fee so the senator could indulge in his eccentric sexual appetite.

Other than a few empty, albeit cordial, comments regarding the senator's absence, not a single guest raised a brow at Steve's being there. He'd become a recognized and respected figure within Washington's tight-knit membership of back stabbers and deal makers.

Rumor had it that the vice president and perhaps even the president were scheduled to make a brief appearance at the party. It never hurt to be seen by two such important men.

Once he had Romine and Douglas silenced, which had better be soon, and Boswell appointed to the Supreme Court, Steve planned to make a request of the senator. For a man having political designs that did not include running for office, there was only so far someone like Steve could rise in his career, but he had plans. Big plans that would take him directly to the top office. And he had more than enough information on the senator to completely ruin the man if he refused to cooperate.

The time had come to put the dirt he had on Phipps to good use, and move on to a bigger and more powerful position...as aide to the vice president of the United States. There was little doubt in Steve's mind that the current president would serve another term. With the growing popularity of the vice president, thanks to his patient rights platform, he was a contender for the big job himself once the president finished his second term in office.

Steve took another sip of champagne as he half listened to a congratulatory speech by the Speaker of the House. Aide to the president of the United States. Better yet, chief of staff. Oh, he really liked the sound of that. Not bad for trailer trash, either, he thought, with a slight inclination of his head in greeting to a freshman senator from New York, who'd arrived late for the party.

The cell phone tucked in the inside pocket of his Armani tuxedo vibrated noiselessly. Under normal circumstances, Steve would ignore it and allow his voice mail to take the call. Only these were not normal circumstances. Not with Romine still on the loose and, he feared, getting closer to the truth.

He walked to the back of the room and slipped into a carpeted hallway. Entering the first door he came to, he stepped inside a private study and closed the door after flipping on the light. "Radcliffe."

"Mr. Radcliffe. Ford Stanton from the *Washington Post*."

Steve's ears started to buzz, a low-sounding hum that slowly took over his body. "How did you get this number?" he demanded, but his voice lacked its usual authority. Only three people had the number to his private cell phone, and a reporter from the *Post* was not one of them.

"Mr. Radcliffe, would you confirm that you provided Attorney William Minor with funds from Senator Phipps, which you authorized for disbursement into accounts held by Justice Department Council Peyton Douglas?"

Steve reached blindly for the floral-patterned wing chair in front of the rich, cherrywood desk. Minor had gone to the papers. That was the only explanation he could come up with to explain how a *Washington Post* reporter knew he was connected to the cover-up. "I have no comment," he said, and quickly disconnected the call.

How the hell had some nobody reporter gotten Minor to talk? Worse, how had the reporter even known of Minor's existence? There was only one answer, and it made the blood in Steve's veins turn to ice water. Jared Romine.

Maybe he was overreacting. Perhaps the reporter

had only been on a fishing expedition. But he'd known about Minor. This was not good.

William Minor had not only been paid handsomely for his services, and his silence, but Steve made sure there was a constant and steady stream of clients sent his way.

No, he thought with a desperate shake of his head. The reporter must've talked to Minor, because there was no way to connect Steve to the filtering of money into the Douglas account without confirmation from the lawyer. He had no idea exactly what Minor had told the reporter, but it sounded as if he'd sung like a goddamn canary.

Steve took a deep breath, then another, before he tucked his cell phone back into the pocket of his tuxedo. He sure hoped the big-mouthed bastard had enjoyed the sunset tonight, because it was definitely going to be his last.

Feeling slightly more in control, he left the quiet study and went to make arrangements for Minor's permanent disappearance.

MOST REPORTERS HAD a string of resources and contacts that even the feds envied, and Ford Stanton was no exception. Producing the private cell number of the aide who had replaced Roland Santiago was nothing short of good networking. Plus, it appeared they'd hit pay dirt with one phone call.

"It's not an official confirmation as far as the story goes," Stanton said, "but it's enough for me to believe that Steven Radcliffe is involved."

Jared couldn't disagree. It made perfect sense. Radcliffe had replaced Santiago, which translated to a job description that included keeping the senator's o little secrets and covering up the senator's indiscretions. Jared already knew Phipps wasn't what he appeared, since he and Dysert had been assigned to investigate the senator over three years ago. What he hadn't understood, however, was that even after Jared's disappearance, there'd never been any word of an investigation of the senator. A clue that had made it obvious to him that someone high up in the bureau had been involved with Phipps, or perhaps even Radcliffe.

"Minor's going to need protection," Jared told Ford. "Immediately. Especially if you're right about this."

Ford sat back in the chair and grinned. "Oh, I'm right, all right. I have a contact or two in the bureau who can make sure Minor isn't harmed."

Jared shook his head. "No! We don't know yet who in the bureau is involved. You make the wrong contact and Minor is as good as dead. The guy deserves to be disbarred for the part he's played, but not killed."

Ford leaned forward and pointed to the papers scattered on the table—documents Jared had brought with him to back up his claim. "Relax, Romine. I know what I'm doing."

Jared didn't like what he believed was Stanton's sudden overconfidence. It hadn't only been lack of information that had kept him on the run for three years, but a lack of trust. Gibson Russell had assigned him and Dysert to the Phipps investigation, and only Gib had known the two of them weren't together the night Dysert and Santiago were killed. Someone high in the bureau was involved—maybe Gib, maybe

The exact identity of the dirty agent
... remain a mystery—a deadly mystery, as
... was concerned.

... d and gathered up the papers, his tapes
and ... "Come on, Romine. We're going for a
ride."

"Ride? Ride where?"

That ever-present grin on Ford's face widened.
"We're going to pay a little visit to Dawson Craig."

Jared couldn't quite believe his ears. "Dawson
Craig? As in Director of the Federal Bureau of Investigation Dawson Craig?"

Ford chuckled. "The one and only."

"Dawson Craig is one of your contacts within the
bureau?" he asked incredulously. In all the years he'd
been with the FBI, even he'd never had any direct
contact with the director himself. The fact that a junior
staff reporter of the *Post* did blew him away.

"Yeah," Ford said with more of that cocksure confidence Jared was slowly beginning to admire. "It really helps when you've got an older sister married to
the old man's son."

A HALF HOUR LATER, two agents personally selected
by Director Dawson Craig were stationed inside William Minor's Arlington, Virginia, home. Minor himself had been moved to protective custody, where he
would remain until Radcliffe was safely under arrest.
And it'd all been ordered from the director's kitchen
table.

Dawson laid his cell phone on the oak table and
gave Jared a hard look, his pale blue eyes missing
nothing. "Okay, I've done as you asked, Agent Rom-

ine, based on the scant information Ford gave me.
Now I want a full explanation, or I will personally
place you under arrest.''

Jared drained his glass of single malt scotch. He'd
expected to either be arrested or shot on sight, not
invited to sit at the director of the bureau's kitchen
table with a glass of whiskey. The fact that he had
said a hell of a lot for the director's faith in Ford
Stanton and his insistence that a lowly Washington
lawyer needed immediate protection.

Starting slowly, Jared reiterated everything he
knew, from the initial investigation into Phipps for
suspected tax fraud, to finding Dysert and Santiago
murdered in Phipps's office. He included his search
of Dysert's apartment and the short list of possible
Supreme Court appointees he'd found. He explained
the years he'd been on the run and his one mistake
that had left a woman dead. He talked of Chase
Bracken and how he'd been given the information regarding Phipps's involvement with the board of directors of certain HMOs who paid the senator big bucks
to protect their interests on the Hill. Money Jared still
believed Phipps continued to receive. He showed the
director the evidence he did have, what he knew as
fact and what he suspected, however circumstantial.
He even went so far as to explain how he'd kidnapped
Peyton in hopes of keeping her safe. By the time he
finished, and sat waiting for the director's reaction,
he'd drained his second glass of scotch.

''That's quite a tale, Agent Romine.''

That was the second time the director had referred
to him as an agent, as if he was still a part of the
bureau. But he wasn't. He'd told Peyton that he could

return to the bureau if the opportunity was still there for him, but hearing himself referred to as Agent Romine sounded foreign to him now. Maybe it was the length of time he'd been underground, or maybe it was something more complicated. He couldn't say. All he knew was that it just didn't feel the same any longer.

"I realize that, sir," Jared said. "I also realize that much of the evidence I have is circumstantial."

"True," Ford added. "But it can be verified. I can verify it."

"You?" Jared asked, glancing in his direction.

The reporter shrugged. "Sure, why not? That way no one has to know the bureau is involved."

The director cleared his throat. "That's not necessary, Ford. The bureau *is* involved, only not as it should be." No one missed the censure in Dawson Craig's voice.

Jared twirled the glass in his hands. "We still don't know who in the bureau is involved."

Ford rested his forearms on the table. "My guess is Gibson Russell."

Jared mulled that over, but the director shook his head. "It's possible, but I have my doubts."

"Why else would the plug have been pulled on the investigation into Phipps?" Ford asked. "Russell is the one who sent Romine and Dysert in, in the first place."

"Gib didn't pull the plug on the Phipps investigation," Dawson explained, his heavy salt-and-pepper brows pulling into a vicious frown.

Jared set his glass down. "Then who did?" he asked.

Dawson smacked his hand on the table. "The same person whom I assigned supervision of the investigation into the president's short list. The same person in charge of the investigation requests of the Senate Judicial Committee, and who has access to the kind of information you brought me."

Jared and Ford both waited, although Ford was just a tad bit more impatient. "Well?" the reporter asked, practically chewing his lips in anticipation.

"Vivien," the director said solemnly.

Ford sat back and let out a low whistle. "The assistant director? The bureau's number two man, er, woman?"

"Vivien Kent?" Jared clarified.

The disappointment on Dawson's face was palpable as he nodded. "Vivien *Galloway* Kent. The daughter of the president's new appointment to the U.S. Supreme Court."

Dawson's cell phone rang, giving Jared a moment to digest the knowledge that Vivien Kent had been pulling the strings all along. He'd had no idea Kent was related to Galloway, especially in a town that practically hummed with gossip.

He glanced over at Ford, who sat scribbling more notes on his legal pad, no doubt envisioning the headlines in tomorrow's newspaper, along with his byline. There were still unanswered questions. Who actually had killed Dysert and Santiago? Jared suspected Radcliffe as the actual trigger man, but considering the shocking news that Kent was involved, he wouldn't put it past her, especially when he took into account the fact that her father had just been appointed to the Supreme Court.

He wondered why Peyton had never mentioned Galloway's daughter. Peyton had worked as his law clerk for quite some time. Was it possible she didn't know Vivien Kent was Theodore Galloway's daughter?

"When?" Dawson asked the caller. After a pause, he added, "I'll be there within the hour."

Jared's interest immediately shifted to Dawson. Something had gone down. He could feel it. A quick glance at Ford, and he realized the reporter knew it, as well, since his pencil had stopped moving.

Dawson looked at Jared, his expression blank. "Make damn sure you keep her alive," he said, then disconnected the call.

He set the phone back on the table and stood. "That was Gib. Seems your girlfriend just turned herself in to one of my agents."

15

PEYTON AND SUNNY WALKED quietly down the Jet-way, with the assistance of a two-man police escort that had been waiting for them at Reagan National. Although she was wearing a pair of handcuffs that had caused innumerable stares and even a few nasty looks tossed her way throughout the flight, only she and Sunny knew the truth. She wasn't officially under arrest, but Chase had suggested they use the legal route to their advantage, since it would get them back to D.C. in a hurry. Their plan had worked, considering it was only a few minutes shy of midnight as they entered the terminal.

Sunny had insisted Chase return to Cole Harbor, since he was no longer an agent and his presence would most assuredly raise suspicion. The plan was to get Peyton to a safe place and keep her there until all the players were behind bars. Chase had argued, but Sunny had been firm. Peyton wished like the devil Chase had accompanied them. Not that she didn't trust Sunny to protect her, but just the muscular appearance of Jared's future brother-in-law would make someone think twice before trying anything.

She still had no idea where Jared was or if he was even safe, and that drove her crazy. As far as she was concerned, the fact that he'd taken off without a word to her stood as testament that he would never change. They'd broken through barriers the night before, but apparently it hadn't been enough for him to stick around when things got a little too emotional.

Had she really expected him to change? She thought about that for a moment and quickly realized the answer was no. The truth was, she'd hoped he'd had, but apparently Jared would always be Jared.

Sunny's steps faltered, drawing Peyton's attention.

"What the hell is she doing here?" Sunny murmured, just loud enough for Peyton to hear.

Peyton followed Sunny's line of vision to a tall willowy blonde waiting with two men in dark suits, obvious agents. The woman wore a sparkly top and black silk pants beneath a black wool coat. Her hair, swept into an updo, was perfectly in place. Obviously, she'd been called away from a party. The woman looked just as elegant as Peyton remembered her. "Vivien Galloway?"

Sunny stopped. With her hand on Peyton's arm, she had no choice but to halt, as well. "You know her?" Sunny asked.

Peyton nodded. "I used to work for her father." She hadn't known Vivien all that well, but the few times she'd been invited to Theodore Galloway's home, she'd had occasion to speak with his daughter. At the time, Vivien had been preparing for her wedding, but Peyton hadn't paid much attention. She was only one of several clerks that worked in Galloway's office and had had no reason to associate with the man's daughter. She'd left Galloway's office and gone on to the Justice Department, and that had been the end of her brief association with Vivien.

"Why would she be here?" Peyton asked.

Sunny cast a quick glance at Vivien and the two waiting agents, who were dismissing the police escort. "Because Vivien *Kent* is the assistant director of the bureau, and the person Gib Russell answers to," Sunny answered hurriedly. "Look, Peyton, this isn't a good sign. I called Gib, not Vivien. There's only one reason she would be here. Do you understand what I'm saying?"

Fear slowly wound its way up Peyton's spine. "My God," she whispered. "She's the inside man Jared has been looking for all this time."

Which meant she, and possibly Sunny, too, were as good as dead.

As THE LINE OF CARS with flashing lights neared the airport, Jared's anticipation mounted. And so did his anger.

He'd honestly believed he'd be beyond anger at this point, he realized as he tapped his foot impatiently on the floorboard of the director's Chevy Suburban. The last thing he wanted to do was jump to conclusions, but Peyton turning herself in to the feds had him wondering about her faith in him. Of course, he had only himself to blame, since he'd taken off without a word. He didn't believe for a minute she'd betrayed him, again, but he couldn't help the slight niggle of doubt.

Still, he'd screwed up. He only hoped that she could forgive him for leaving her without so much as a hint of his plans, or not telling her if he'd be returning anytime soon.

The ringing of the director's cell phone cut into his thoughts. The call was brief. "That was Gib," Dawson said, tossing the phone back onto the console as they sped along the freeway toward the airport, followed by three other vehicles filled with federal agents. "They caught a couple of goons trying to break into Minor's house. They gave up Radcliffe, and he's being arrested as we speak."

It would be over soon, of that Jared was certain. And then what? he wondered.

"What about Kent?" Ford Stanton asked from the back seat.

"Nothing," Dawson answered. "Gib hasn't heard from the two agents he sent to bring her in."

The anticipation coursing through Jared's veins picked up speed. He had a bad feeling Kent might have found out Agent MacGregor and Peyton were flying in and had gone to the airport to meet them. If she got to them before they did, he didn't want to think about what could happen to Peyton.

"Thank you, Agent MacGregor. I'll take over from here."

Peyton wished Sunny had removed the handcuffs, but at least her hands were bound in front of her rather than behind her back. Of course, with two burly, armed agents present, she wouldn't get very far if she did try to run.

"Special Agent Russell is waiting for me to bring in Ms. Douglas, ma'am," Sunny said. "He's expecting us."

Vivien's icy blue eyes narrowed suspiciously, chilling Peyton's blood. Sunny was right; Vivien was involved.

"Watch her," Vivien said coldly to the two other agents. "MacGregor, come with me please."

"Ma'am, I really don't—"

"Are you attempting to defy a direct order, Agent MacGregor?"

Sunny bit her lip. "No, ma'am," she said eventually.

"I didn't think so." Without so much as a glance in Peyton's direction, Vivien turned and indicated that Sunny should precede her across the near-empty terminal to the ladies' room.

The two women slipped inside. Peyton's heart rate accelerated. Whether she attempted an escape or not, they were going to kill her, of that she had little doubt. That being the case, she had nothing to lose by trying to make a run for it.

The two agents, both of whom stood directly in front of her, stared down at her, their faces impassive. With her jacket over her hands, she had to wonder if they even knew she was cuffed. Not that it would make a difference when they gunned her down for a botched escape attempt.

She gathered up her courage, but it was too late. Vivien exited the ladies' room, without Sunny MacGregor.

"It's been a long time, Peyton," Vivien said with a cool smile once she rejoined her thugs. "I'd ask how you've been, but I think that's rather obvious."

Vivien was a good five to ten years older than Peyton. Time, and what Peyton was sure had been a long parade of cosmetic professionals, had been good to her.

"Daddy must be so proud," Peyton spat at her. "I

wonder, how do you think he's going to feel knowing his daughter would stoop to criminal activity to see him seated on the bench?''

Her smile faded. ''My father's future is secure. And no one will be the wiser, once you and Romine are out of the way.'' She paused, no doubt for effect. ''Speaking of which, just where is your boyfriend, Peyton? Did he run off on you again?''

If her hands weren't cuffed, she might have punched Vivien right in her perfect nose.

Vivien grabbed Peyton by the upper arm and started walking her through the nearly deserted terminal. The two agents maintained an even pace a few feet behind them.

''Since you're going to kill me anyway,'' Peyton said, in what she hoped was not a vain attempt to buy time until she could figure out a way to escape Vivien and her henchmen, ''answer a couple of questions for me.''

Vivien sighed. ''Is this chatter really necessary?''

Peyton ignored the snide comment. ''What's in all this for you, other than handing Daddy a seat on the Supreme Court?''

Vivien laughed. ''Are you really all that naive, Peyton?''

Peyton shrugged. ''Money usually plays a role somewhere.''

''Money doesn't interest me.''

''Power, then.''

''Perhaps you're not as stupid as I give you credit for being. With my father on the bench, they wouldn't dare pass me over for the director's job.''

''The director's job? He'd have to step down

first…'' The import of Vivien's words hit her with the force of a hurricane. The director wouldn't be stepping down, he'd be eliminated—by Vivien or someone under her control. Good God, was there no end to the nightmare she and Jared and been pulled into?

They reached the end of the first concourse and turned right. To Peyton's relief, a flurry of men in blue suits charged toward them, guns drawn. Her joy was short-lived when the goons behind her rushed forward, their own weapons drawn.

"It's over, Vivien," someone shouted.

"Let her go!" another, more familiar voice called out, raising Peyton's hopes that she would get out of this alive. Jared.

Looking for him, Peyton searched the faces of the agents scattered in front of them. He walked slowly toward them, moving easily past the others. God, she'd never been happier to see another human being in her life.

"Let her go, Vivien." The owner of the first voice she'd heard materialized—an older gentleman she vaguely recognized from somewhere. "Do you really want to add another murder charge to those already against you?"

Vivien stopped and jostled Peyton to keep her in front of her. "You have nothing on me, Dawson. Nothing."

"You're wrong, Vivien," the man stated in a calm, authoritative voice. Peyton finally recognized him as Dawson Craig, the FBI's top man. "We have plenty. Murder, conspiracy, conspiracy to commit murder, fraud, obstruction of justice. Shall I continue?"

Vivien's attention remained on the director, but

Peyton couldn't take her eyes off of Jared as he continued to move toward them.

Something hard suddenly pressed against her ribs. This was no disposable lighter. She had no trouble recognizing the cold steel barrel of the gun Vivien held on her.

Jared inched closer.

Vivien swung around and aimed the gun right at Jared's chest.

From somewhere behind him, someone yelled, "Freeze!" but Vivien ignored the order and pulled the trigger.

Bullets started flying. They whizzed past Peyton and pinged against doors and security gates. She heard a grunt as one of Vivien's men hit the ground with a thud. Peyton looked down into his unseeing eyes and nearly lost her fried-chicken dinner.

She wanted to duck, hit the floor, dive for cover before she joined the dead agent, but Vivien's excruciating grip on her arm kept her upright, a human shield.

The second of Vivien's henchmen hit the floor. Her hold on Peyton tightened as she slowly began to move backward through the concourse.

Jared dove for them, and Vivien fired again. He appeared to stop in midair, his body twisting in a frightening display as he fell to the ground.

"Jared!" Peyton screamed just as another shot rang out. Vivien's grip on her loosened. Peyton twisted away and ran to Jared as Vivien crumpled to the floor.

Peyton's heart pounded wildly as she knelt beside Jared, hoping, praying that he would survive. Blood oozed from his side, soaking his shirt. He was unconscious, but breathing, and for now that had to be enough, because she knew clear down to her soul there was no way she could lose Jared a second time and survive the heartache.

FINGERS OF EARLY MORNING light crept through the opening in the heavy drapes covering the window of Jared's hospital room at Bethesda Medical Center on Tuesday morning. It'd been six hours since the incident at the airport, and slowly Peyton had started to relax.

She pushed aside the blanket a kindly nurse had given her as she'd hovered between wakefulness and light sleep while she held vigil in the hard vinyl chair next to Jared's bed. They'd had to perform surgery to remove the bullet, which had entered his side and, thankfully, been stopped by a rib, preventing further, and possibly fatal, damage. After a few weeks of recovery, he would be back on his feet and able to return to his job at the bureau, if that was truly what he decided he wanted.

She'd already contacted her boss at the Justice Department and made arrangements for a leave of absence. Under the circumstances, her boss hadn't argued, and had promised to make sure her cases were covered.

There was no doubt in her mind where Jared would spend the next six weeks of recovery—in her home where she could keep a close eye on him. Some might say she was being overprotective, but the truth went far deeper. She had no intention of letting him out of her sight until she was confident he would be okay. Once he recovered, they could begin to discuss the future and whether or not it included them being together.

For those brief seconds when she'd feared Vivien had killed Jared, Peyton had realized her life would once again be hollow without him. She'd spent the past three years with him never far from her thoughts, and while she'd tried to move on with her life, she knew she'd only been going through the motions. Oh, sure, the two of them had a few issues to work through, but she didn't believe for a second they couldn't overcome a few more hurdles. She firmly believed that if their relationship was strong, they could handle together whatever came their way.

Jared's former boss, Gibson Russell, had remained at the hospital until Jared had come out of surgery and he personally heard the okay from the doctors that Jared would have a full recovery. While much of Gib's attention had been on the various phone calls coming in on his cell phone, plus checking on Sunny MacGregor, Peyton had still appreciated his presence.

Sunny was due to be released later this afternoon. She'd suffered a concussion and a few ugly bruises to the side of her face and back of her head thanks to Vivien pistol-whipping her into unconsciousness in the airport ladies' room. Sunny had come around long enough to make her way down the concourse, and had been the one to fire the shot that had stopped Vivien. After firing her weapon, Sunny had passed out again, but other than a headache and those bruises, she, too, would see a full recovery.

Vivien Kent wouldn't be quite so lucky. Oh, she would recover from the gunshot wound to her right shoulder, but she'd be doing so in a federal prison until the legal system finished with her.

Slowly, all the pieces had fallen together to form the big picture. Apparently, Roland Santiago had murdered Jared's partner when Dysert had confronted the aide about the president's short list of candidates for possible Supreme Court justice appointments. Santiago had panicked and had contacted Vivien, who'd been on Phipps's payroll since her days as a field agent. When Santiago had begun making noises about being in over their heads and coming out with the truth, Vivien had killed him. She was also the one responsible for Beth's murder.

Steven Radcliffe, someone Peyton had never heard of until Gib Russell explained his association with Senator Martin Phipps, was guilty of several conspiracy charges, including conspiracy to murder, fraud and obstruction of justice. He'd initiated the cover-up of Santiago's and Dysert's murders, had planted the money she'd been accused of receiving from Jared, and had been instrumental in fraudulent background investigations that had eliminated several upstanding candidates from the president's short list to ensure the HMO cases coming before the Supreme Court would not be heard. In exchange for a lighter sentence, Radcliffe had given up every bit of information surrounding the hell Jared had been put through for the past three years. The shake-up of the political arena would be vast as the investigations continued, Gib had explained to her while they'd waited for word on Jared. Russell had even gone so far as to estimate several long-standing political careers would no doubt be ruined, starting with Senator Phipps's. The public might be able to forgive Phipps for being arrested in the arms of a high-dollar prostitute, but even in today's political climate, a conspiracy to set the balance of the high court in order to keep his pockets lined with kickback money was something citizens, and especially Phipps's political opponents, would not soon forget.

The heavy wood door swung open just as Peyton stood to work out the kink in her back caused by her cramped position in the chair. Instead of more thermometer-and-blood-pressure-cuff-wielding nurses, or a visit from Jared's surgeon, as she'd expected, Leland Atwood filled the doorway.

He let the door close behind him as he stepped into the room. "I had a feeling I'd find you here," he said quietly and without censure. "I came as soon as I heard the news."

Her gaze shot to Jared, who continued to sleep peacefully under the residual affects of the anesthesia, then back to Leland. Seeing them together, she was struck by the similarities in the two men. They were roughly the same height and coloring, but the comparisons went beyond a physical resemblance. She finally understood what had attracted her to Leland in the first place, and was deeply saddened to realize her emotional attachment to him stemmed from the fact that he'd reminded her of Jared, albeit subconsciously. While she might have told Jared over and over again how different Leland was from him, she'd really been in a deep state of denial that had served a purpose in protecting her heart. Their honorable nature and their deep belief that justice would always prevail, with the help of the good guys, was startlingly similar. She couldn't help feeling guilty as she realized now that

Leland had only been a substitute for what she really wanted all along—Jared. She *had* loved Leland, but not in the way he'd wanted, or deserved, to be loved. She couldn't, not when she'd never stopped loving Jared. That little bit of honesty didn't make her feel a whole lot better about herself, either.

"Are you all right?" Leland asked as he crossed the room toward her.

"I'll be fine," she told him.

He stopped in front of her. "You could've come to me." He reached out and cupped her cheek in his warm palm.

Instead of turning to the warmth and comfort he offered, she pulled away. Yes, she realized now, she probably could have gone to him, and she understood he would've moved heaven and earth to clear her name, regardless of the disruption it would have created in his own orderly world. But that wouldn't have been fair to either of them, not when her heart had always belonged to another.

She cleared her throat. "Leland, I'm sorry. I never meant for any of this to happen."

He stuffed his hands in the front pockets of his slacks and offered her a rueful smile. "I know," he said gently. The understanding in his dark brown eyes heightened her guilt over the pain she was sure she was causing him. "I just came to see for myself that you were all right...and to say goodbye."

The sting of tears blurred her vision. She tried to blink them back, and failed.

She reached inside her pocket and pulled out the engagement ring he'd given her the night before Jared had returned to her life and ruthlessly reclaimed her heart, her body and her soul. "I think this belongs to you," she said, taking his hand and setting the ring in his palm.

His fingers closed around it and he smiled in that gentle way of his. "We could have had a good life together, Peyton. You know that, don't you?"

Her throat burned with the tears she tried to withhold. "I know," she admitted in a choked whisper. Leland may have been a good choice for her, but he wasn't the choice her heart had made. That was a decision that had been taken out of her hands by the love of another man many years before.

You can't choose who you fall in love with. No words could have rung more true for her at this moment.

He lifted his hand and rubbed the pad of his thumb along her cheek. His own eyes were suspiciously bright. "Don't cry," he told her. "You should be happy. Most people only have one chance to find true love. You've been given a second chance, Peyton. Make the best of it."

He leaned toward her and placed a tender kiss on her cheek. Turning, he walked out of her life, and never looked back.

She turned to the window and stared at the horizon, now bright with the kiss of morning sunshine. Pulling in a shaky breath, she let it out slowly as she struggled to keep more tears at bay. Leland may not have been the *one,* but that didn't mean she didn't feel a sense of loss.

A movement from the bed caught her attention. She looked over her shoulder and right into Jared's green eyes. He looked a little groggy, but alert enough to know what was going on around him.

She turned and propped her backside against the window ledge. "I take it you heard that," she said, folding her arms over her chest. The cad, eavesdropping on such a personal conversation, even if it had taken place at the foot of his bed.

A slow grin spread across his delicious mouth. "Every last word." His voice, while scratchy, still made her pulse pick up speed. "Atwood was a hell of a lot more understanding than I would've been."

She shook her head and pushed away from the window. "I told you he was a good guy." She stopped at the foot of the bed and smiled down at the man who'd stolen her heart and refused to give it back.

His grin turned wicked. "Yeah, but good guys don't turn you on."

"How are you feeling?" she asked, hoping to change the subject. "Are you in pain?"

A frown puckered his brow. "Hell, yes, I'm in pain. I was shot, you know."

"Hmm, yes, I do know." She slowly made her way to the side of the bed. The railing came down easily and she sat carefully beside him. "And you scared me to death. I thought I'd finally lost you for good."

He reached for her hand and brought it to his lips. "Ah, sweetheart, there wasn't a snowball's chance of that happening."

She appreciated his attempt to lighten her fears, but nothing could change the fact that she'd suffered a staggering blow when he'd been shot. "So where do we go from here, Jared?"

"You know, I just happened to be thinking about

that when Atwood walked in the door. I guess since he dumped you, that means I should probably marry you so you can save face.''

Despite the lightness of his tone, his eyes spoke of another emotion, one that ran much deeper and into serious terrain. The truth of the matter was, regardless of the severity of the situation, she appreciated this side of him, the one she hadn't seen in far too long. The one that teased and appeared on the surface to never take anything too seriously. But his eyes told her another story, one that included a lifetime together now that the horrible nightmare their lives had become had finally drawn to a close.

She smoothed a lock of sable hair from his forehead. ''Think we can wait a little while before making that kind of decision, or were you ready to call a priest?''

''Big wedding, huh?''

She'd marry him in a parking garage, if he wanted the truth. ''No. It's just that…well, nothing has changed,'' she said, straightening. ''You left and didn't even have the decency to tell me you were leaving, where you were going, or even what you were planning. Nothing, Jared. Not a single word other than to tell Harry to baby-sit me while you traipsed off to save the day all by yourself. Do you know what that does to a person with severe abandonment issues?''

''I'm sorry,'' he said, and she knew that he meant it. But that still didn't change the fact that he'd frightened her and left her worrying—again.

''It's something I'll have to work on,'' he admitted sheepishly.

''Do you have any idea what I went through?'' she

told him, suddenly angry with him.
seconds when I thought Vivien had
inside, all over again. How many m   246   cauti
expect me to go through this with y   sh

He grinned. She wanted to strangl

"Does that mean you won't marry me?

"Oh, Jared. Can't you be serious for just a minute?"

"Sweetheart, I think we've both had a little too much seriousness the past couple of days," he said. "Marry me, Peyton. Let's spend the rest of our lives loving each other and making up for the time we lost."

She picked up the hand free of an IV needle and laced their fingers together. "That's my problem, Jared," she said in a more reasonable tone. "I do love you. I love you so much I'm terrified of losing you all over again."

His fingers squeezed hers reassuringly. "Baby, I can't give you any guarantees, no more than you can guarantee me that something won't happen to you. No one can do that. Do you really want to spend the rest of your life afraid to take a chance because of what might or might not happen?"

She really, *really* hated it when he was right. She couldn't even find a decent argument against his reasoning. Did she really want to let her fears cripple her to the point they were all she'd have for company in her old age, along with long, lonely nights spent wondering what if? That wasn't living, not by any stretch of the imagination.

She knew the grin she gave him was filled with

..., but she couldn't help it. "One day at a time," told him. "It's all I can give you right now."

He tugged on her hand and urged her mouth closer to his. "As long as you spend every one of those days with me, you got yourself a deal."

He drew their lips together in a kiss, one of those toe-curling numbers that made it impossible for her to resist him. And she wouldn't. She couldn't. Because that was one segment of their history together she never had any intention of changing.

Epilogue

One week later

JARED STILL HADN'T MADE any decisions about returning to his old job at the bureau, although Gib and Dawson Craig assured him the job was there if he still wanted it. He admitted to being tempted, but maybe it was time he stopped putting his life on the line. Still, he had no clue yet what he'd do if he didn't continue with a career in law enforcement.

The week he'd been forced to remain in the hospital, Peyton had been by his side most of the time. When she started looking a little worse for wear, he'd insisted she go home and get some much needed rest of her own. She had argued, but finally relented, only to return before the sun rose the following morning.

"I think we need a bigger car," he said, as Peyton took the exit that would take them to her home in Arlington. "I got used to that truck we stole."

She smiled at him, then shifted her attention to the road. "I happen to like my car, and was grateful to have it returned to me. Besides, since we turned over the money in those fraudulent accounts to the government, I think one of those big Expeditions is a little out of our price range."

It was his turn to smile, and not just because she

continued to refer to them as a couple. "Didn't I tell you? There's a little matter of back pay that apparently the government feels is owed to me."

"How on earth did you manage that?"

He reached over the seat for her hand. "It helps to have friends in high places." It also meant he'd have enough money to make a fresh start even if he chose not to remain with the FBI. Something else to consider, he mused as Peyton made the last turn onto the street where she lived.

She pulled into the driveway next to a dark Ford truck. He didn't have time to ask about the vehicle in the driveway as the front door to Peyton's house swung open and his sister, Dee, emerged. Chase followed not far behind.

"My God," Jared whispered. "She's really here?"

Peyton nodded. "She wanted to be here when you came home."

Home. A word he'd thought for too long would never belong in his vocabulary again. His heart overflowed with love for the woman beside him. "I love you, Peyton."

She offered up a watery smile as tears moistened her eyes. "I know," she said. "I really, *really* know."

He leaned over and kissed her quickly before his sister yanked open the car door and assisted him from the vehicle.

Dee's arms surrounded him and she held on tight. "Thank God you're alive," she whispered. "I think the past few weeks have been the worst."

He held Dee, afraid to let go for fear he'd wake up to find the last days were nothing but a vivid dream. They'd seen each other for the first time in months only a few weeks ago, but this was the first time since the nightmare began that he'd been able to see her and talk to her without fearing for both of their lives. He had Chase to thank for putting his own butt on the line by giving him the information he needed to finally put the past to rest.

Jared pulled back and looked down at Dee. Tears stained her cheeks, and he smiled. "Hey, what's this? Romines don't cry."

She laughed and shook her head. "They most certainly do, especially when they're as happy as I am right now."

His own throat felt more than a little raw and thick at the moment.

Dee sobered as she looked up at him. "You know, Jared, Mom and Dad weren't right about everything. We aren't islands. Even Romines need someone once in a while."

"Amen to that," he said. With his arm still around his sister's shoulders, he turned toward Chase and Peyton. "Have you met my future bride?"

"I haven't agreed just yet," Peyton said, but the loving glance she tossed his way said what her words did not. She loved him and there was no way she was letting him out of her sight. The thought warmed him considerably.

"We've met," Dee told him. "You did good, Brother."

"I couldn't have done it without a little help from my friends." He let go of Dee to shake Chase's hand. During his hospital stay, Peyton had told him about Dee's engagement to Chase, and his involvement in bringing an end to the nightmare that had consumed their lives for far too long. In Jared's opinion, Dee had made a wise choice.

"What do you say we go inside," Jared suggested. There was a small crowd gathering across the street, and he really wanted to have some privacy with the people he loved and cared about. "I haven't even seen where I'm going to be living yet."

"That's something else we haven't agreed upon," Peyton said, moving toward him.

Dee laughed and slipped her arms around Chase's waist. "You might as well give in, Peyton. You'll never survive being seduced by the enemy. I know I didn't stand a chance."

Jared wasn't worried. He knew Peyton would marry him, just as he knew deep in his heart they'd spend the rest of their lives together. They were fated to be together, and no one, not even a gorgeous, stubborn lawyer who'd stolen his heart, could argue with fate.

Together the four of them walked toward the house. "She doesn't want to give up her maiden name," Jared said.

"That's not true," Peyton said, helping him up the brick steps. Not that he needed assistance, but he wasn't about to let her know it.

"Sweetheart, I don't mind if you hyphenate," he teased, and laughed when Peyton rolled her eyes as they stepped inside the house. Together. Because Dee was right. Romines weren't islands. They needed someone to love just like the rest of humanity.

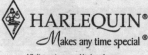

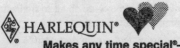

HARLEQUIN®
Temptation.

Look for bed, breakfast and more...!

Some of your favorite Temptation authors are checking in early at Cooper's Corner Bed and Breakfast

In May 2002:

#877 The Baby and the Bachelor
Kristine Rolofson

In June 2002:

#881 Double Exposure
Vicki Lewis Thompson

In July 2002:

#885 For the Love of Nick
Jill Shalvis

In August 2002 things heat up even more at Cooper's Corner. There's a whole year of intrigue and excitement to come—twelve fabulous books bound to capture your heart and mind!

Join all your favorite Harlequin authors in Cooper's Corner!

HARLEQUIN®
Makes any time special ®

Visit us at www.eHarlequin.com

HTCC